Dutch Kangaroo

A tale of actions and reactions

Katja Bongers

Grosvenor House
Publishing Limited

All rights reserved
First published in Dutch in January 2023
Original title: *Kangoeroe in de Polder (Actie is Reactie)*
Copyright © Katja Bongers, 2023

The right of Katja Bongers to be identified as the author of this
work has been asserted in accordance with Section 78
of the Copyright, Designs and Patents Act 1988

The book cover is copyright to Katja Bongers

This book is published by
Grosvenor House Publishing Ltd
Link House
140 The Broadway, Tolworth, Surrey, KT6 7HT.
www.grosvenorhousepublishing.co.uk

This book is sold subject to the conditions that it shall not, by way of
trade or otherwise, be lent, resold, hired out or otherwise circulated
without the author's or publisher's prior consent in any form of binding or
cover other than that in which it is published and
without a similar condition including this condition being imposed
on the subsequent purchaser.

This book is a work of fiction. Any resemblance to
people or events, past or present, is purely coincidental.

A CIP record for this book
is available from the British Library

ISBN 978-1-80381-466-7

*If two bodies exert forces on each other, these forces have the same magnitude, but opposite directions.
(Sir Isaac Newton's third law of motion)*

1 Action & reaction

2 February, 1986 – Wibautstraat police station

'So, you were not?' The police officer looked at me disparagingly. 'Well?'

Yikes. 'If you put it that way, no,' I said.

'Well, then there's nothing we can do for you. And no, you cannot file a report or even a complaint, and nothing will be put on record, not a syllable, let's be clear about that. There is no criminal offense here, there is no perpetrator, and you are not a victim. And by the way, your mother can come to us herself if she feels the need. Goodbye.'

He half got up, straightened his uniform jacket, leaned over the cluttered desk, and held out his hand to me in farewell. I had already pressed it before I knew it. The word 'victim' reverberated in my brain, and I tasted it in my mind like a foul morsel, making me nauseous.

'Geert, you can't do that,' the female officer whispered to her colleague. 'This isn't about you or what you might think or feel about what she told us. The girl needs our help.' She walked with him towards the door.

'Goddamn it, don't interfere, you bitch. She's been here so many times, I'm completely fed up. Just go away. Get to your real work, that's what I'm doing. And get rid of that chick right away. IMMEDIATELY!' He made no attempt to speak softly, almost was shouting. After all, he was in his rights and I – and everyone else, for that matter – should know it.

Geert stormed out of the room and pulled the door shut behind him, jerking it so hard it banged. You could hear him angrily legging away down the corridor, where doors opened and closed and surprised voices sounded. The female officer raised her eyebrows in exasperation, told me to wait a moment, and ran after him in a hurry. It seemed like an eternity before she returned. And I just sat there, overwhelmed and indecisive. I don't remember what I had actually expected, but certainly not this.

After a few minutes, the female officer came back into the room. She was red in the face and was clearly having trouble breathing calmly. She sat down next to me in the other chair – the one with the peeling paint and faint stains on the seat, which had seemed so dirty I had sat down on the other one. That one had seemed a fraction cleaner but had no armrests.

I picked at the mud on my trousers. They had been splashed with mud on the way to the station when a large truck had driven through a deep puddle on the road next to me. I tried to focus on that moment, so I could be angry about something that had nothing to do with the here and now.

After a long silence, the officer put her hand on mine, and I couldn't ignore her anymore. She looked at me questioningly. 'Can you manage to cycle home alone, dear? Or do you want to wait a while? I'm on duty until ten, and then I can cycle with you. Would you like that?'

I swallowed hard and wiped my sleeve across my face, shaking my head. I didn't know what difference that would make. What good was an officer who would cycle with me? I'm sure it was well-intentioned, but that's not what I had come to the station for.

'Thank you, ma'am,' I whispered, 'there's no need.'

'You don't have to call me madam, my name is Ria.' She gently patted my knee and handed me another tissue. Then she handed me a cup of water, and we sat together for a while without saying anything. When she stood up in silence, I followed her to the reception desk. I too said nothing. Everything had already been said.

Two minutes later, I was in the passage next to the police station, fiddling with my bike. The lock was not cooperating and it was taking too long. The passage stank pungently of piss. I was hot, sweat stung under my armpits, and I was becoming more and more nauseous. Retching, I just managed to undo the lock and to cycle away without breaking my neck. I took deep breaths and tried to breathe in the fresh air as quickly as possible. But a little further on, I had to stop. I threw my bike on the ground, staggered towards the curb, and sat down on it. I stared blankly ahead.

For how long I sat there, I don't remember, but the Amsterdam night was pitch dark. The streetlights had long been on, and there were few people left on the streets. The cold had crept up my legs, and I stood up stiffly. Carefully, I bent my arms and legs strenuously a few times. Ahead, my bike was still on the cycle path. Other cyclists had neatly driven around it, as if it was perfectly normal to have a bicycle in the middle of the path.

I walked over to my bike and put it upright, pressed the dynamo button, and got on. At a reasonable speed I rode down Wibautstraat towards the Amstel train station, past the *Volkskrant* newspaper building on my right, then left towards the student flat where I had been living for a few months. My front light blinked in time with the slipping dynamo.

Back home, I dropped the bike off in the bike cellar and snuck to my room unseen. Thank God I didn't have to face anyone.

In the hot shower, I scrubbed my entire body with the nail brush and lathered my hair three times before rinsing off and getting into bed with clean clothes on. I carefully avoided touching the bruise on my ribs. Nor did I look in the mirror above the sink. In fact, I hadn't done that in weeks.

As for what happened last week, the week before, or even longer ago, we are not going to pay attention to that now. If you don't need hospital treatment, then you haven't been abused. And if you weren't penetrated ('with a cock, a finger, or anything else in your cunt, ass, or mouth,' Officer Geert had snarled), then you have not been raped. So then there is no offense.

And here I was, brought up to think that we had such a fine rule of law in the Netherlands, that we were so nicely emancipated, and that women had the same rights as men. The police were your best friend, indeed. Curled up under the covers, I tried to sleep, or at least try to get warm again. Only my nose stuck out from under the covers.

With a jolt, I woke up. According to the alarm clock, it was three o'clock, but it felt like it was already morning. That was probably because of the huge thirst and hunger that I was now beginning to feel. For days, I had been eating and drinking little.

Greedily, I drank three glasses of water, filling the glass for my toothbrush at the sink. It tasted metallic, but the thirst was gone. The hunger was not. Would I dare to go to the kitchen? I could look in the cupboards there to see if there was anything edible. Usually, the cupboard doors were unlocked, and fellow students would have something there that I could quickly put in my pocket and eat it in my room. I had nothing edible myself. I did have two tea bags and some ground coffee, but no filter. Or would there still be something somewhere so I didn't have to venture into the kitchen? I decided I'd better have a good look around my own room first.

Crouching down, I found a boiled sweet in the back of my desk drawer. A bit old and dusty, but still quite edible. I picked the sweet from its white wrapper and put it in my mouth. Slowly I let it melt on my tongue. Delicious.

In my jacket pocket I found the two packaged lumps of sugar that Officer Geert had given me with my cup of coffee. I ate those too, standing up. That was all, except for a can of tuna and one of tomato puree. I couldn't open those, because I didn't have a can opener in my room. I set the two cans on the edge of my desk. What could I do now? Go to the kitchen? Carefully, I opened my room door and looked to see if anyone was in the corridor. On stockinged feet, I crept towards the kitchen, hoping not to run into anyone.

'Hehe, look who we have here, our little sunshine,' said Wieger, as I opened the door of the fridge. I was startled and hit my head on a kitchen cabinet when I shot upright. The fridge's interior light illuminated the room a little, and I saw that he was sitting in the dark corner by the window. A bottle of cheap gin and a bowl of crisps were on the table in front of him.

'Aaaaaah, poooooor you, bumping your little head like that. Would our shy pussycat like a sip of this goodie for the pain?' he asked, holding up the bottle. 'Come and sit on Uncle Wieger's lap then, won't you? Then I'll gently stroke that bump on your brow. Or any other bump, hehehe.'

I thought he was a jerk, so I tried to ignore him. Now, though, I couldn't check the kitchen cupboards unseen for anything edible.

Wieger's crisps looked delicious to me and it looked like the bowl was still half-full. He could keep that gin, but maybe...

'But wait, you are a teetotaler, I almost forgot,' said Wieger. With a wicked look, he poured the last of the gin into his mouth, wiped it circumstantially, let out a popping belch, then left the kitchen without giving me a single glance. The bowl of crisps remained behind. I grabbed it from the table when I heard his room door slam shut and took it to my room.

May 1963 – About men

'Men are all lechers, and they only want one thing.' As a young girl, Mum got this warning regularly from her mother. Apparently, it made an impression, because before she met him, she never had a boyfriend. She was a nurse from a Roman Catholic family from the south of the country.

When she was fourteen, her mother took her to the nuns at the hospital in Roermond, to scrub the floors as a maid for a pittance. As an intern she was allowed to go home only every other weekend.

Despite her homesickness, she managed to stand out from the other maids there, and the nuns saw that she had more to offer. At the intercession of the nuns and at the parish's expense, she received training to be a 'sister', as nurses were then still being called in the Netherlands. She lived in a big boarding house with all the other sisters. They were all apparently sexless women, who clenched their knees chastely when men were around.

At the age of twenty-two she moved to Deventer, where she started working in the neurology department of the local hospital. There, she saw her first naked man – a patient she had to help wash. She could still recount that shock with horror years later.

At a dance night for nurses, she met him (an apparently shy metal worker who also came to watch the dancing) by chance. With her soft singsong southern accent and her nurse's uniform, she was very attractive to him. Jealously, he kept a close eye on all the other men who were ogling her.

Their relationship until their marriage was very chaste; at most there was some kissing and hand-holding, but nothing else. And after their marriage day, they experienced nothing exciting together in the big bed. He had his rights, Mum submitted to her marital duty... or something like that. But surely something had really happened between the two, otherwise they would not have had children.

Much later, her daughter nearly choked on tuna canape when a friend announced during a dinner party that her parents had not had the best sex life together. She articulated this by saying about her parents, 'Aaaah, he turned her over and he had his way with her.' The girl's boyfriend took another bite of macaroni and said cheerfully, 'Gosh, you'd kill for that, wouldn't you?'

3 February, 1986 – Mistress of my own money

Somewhere mid-morning, after the usual noisy morning ritual of breakfasting and departing fellow residents, the corridor was quiet again. After listening with my ear to the door for a few minutes to see if the coast was clear, I dared to walk to the kitchen again. Fortunately, no one else was there now, so I could inspect all the cupboards without getting caught.

My loot consisted of one slice of bread, a limp cracker, and some jam, which I spread straight from the jar I had found in Fenna's cupboard onto the bread and the cracker. With one of my remaining tea bags and some sugar from the communal pot on the dining table, I also made a big cup of tea. Unfortunately, there was no milk in the fridge, except for an open carton with a distinctly sour smell. Wieger's note ('KEEP YOUR FUCKING HANDS OFF MY MILK!') had worked.

Breakfast gave me new energy. In my room, I checked how much money I had left. Two guilders, a quarter, two dimes, and a penny. I knew I should be able to buy food with this, but for how many days? And on Mondays, Jac Hermans' supermarket did not open until one o'clock, still hours away. And what would I do once everything was gone? There was nothing left in my checking account either. And he had been crystal clear: If I didn't come home, I wouldn't get any household money. I had to think of a way to get more money.

Just as the temp agency opened, I stood at the door, freshly washed and combed and in my neatest clothes. It was quite windy out there on the Heiligeweg, and I hoped my hair would stay tidy enough to make a good first impression.

I told the intermediary (I had never heard of that job title before) that I could type well, that I was a student looking for a part-time job because my parents didn't give me enough money to make ends meet, and that I wanted to be independent. She looked me up and down with a pinched mouth, on which she had applied bright red lipstick while I was speaking. From my somewhat windswept but clean hair to my simple but neat clothes, to my well-polished shoes, she looked at everything carefully, without any embarrassment. Apparently, I passed her test, because now I could get a little smile from the red lips. I was sure she saw a provincial girl; ordinary, but neat.

A typing test I could do right away. The intermediary looked over my shoulder to see how I was doing, and I think she also inspected my nails to make sure that they were clean. Fortunately, I managed to achieve the minimum number of keystrokes required on the rickety office machine to be able to hire me as an administrative assistant.

'When could you start?' she asked.

'Today, ma'am, but preferably in the afternoons or on weekends, so I don't miss any lectures.'

Pondering, she looked at me, picked up the phone, and dialed a number then chattered a bit to the person on the other end. She sounded artificially cheerful, but apparently she was successful.

After a short conversation, she put down the receiver. 'OK. Here's the deal,' she said. 'You can start next week as an administrative assistant at the Municipal Insurance Department. Every working day from three to six. We'll pay you three guilders and eighty-five cents per hour, including taxes. But if you're late, or don't do a good job, you'll be out on your ear in a second. And you must hand in your signed worksheets here promptly by the end of every week. Understood?'

'Yes, thank you very much, ma'am.' I didn't know what she meant by those worksheets, but I didn't dare ask about them. I would find out later.

Excited, I cycled back home. A pity, though, that I would not get my first pay sooner than next week. That did bother me a bit. How was I going to manage in the meantime? I quickly cycled past Wibautstraat police station towards Jac Hermans' supermarket. There I waited in front of the doors for it to open, huddled with other people who were already standing around.

Once inside, I managed to get a loaf of bread, a packet of margarine, a big bag of macaroni, a packet of tea, two tomatoes, an onion ('Well, well, we're having a shopping spree today,' the boy from the vegetable department said sarcastically), and to buy a litre of yogurt, all within my budget of two guilders and fifty cents. I even got two cents in change.

I stuffed my own receipt and any other receipts I could find at the checkout along with my purchases in my shopping bag.

With the macaroni, the tomatoes, and the onion, the cans of tuna and tomato puree, half a packet of margarine, and some spices that I stole from Wieger's cupboard, I prepared a large pan of food, from which I ate a plateful every day. The bread I spread with the rest of the margarine and jam from my fellow students' cupboards, and the yoghurt I ate in small portions with sugar from the communal pot.

The food was boring and bland, and after three days I was truly sick of the macaroni. I longed for a good meal, and even the mash of sauerkraut that Wieger was warming up on Wednesday evening smelt delicious. So did the smoked sausage he had with it. But he unfortunately ate everything himself. Only the two small pieces of meat on the string of the smoked sausage, which he had cut off and left on the kitchen counter, I was able to appropriate unseen.

On Thursday morning, the rubbish was collected, and I got up extra early to put out our rubbish bag. I handed in all the glass jars and bottles that my fellow residents had carelessly thrown in at the supermarket, and I bought two apples and a tin of tomato soup with the deposit. All in all, I wasn't really hungry, but I craved a big pile of tasty, fresh food.

I had to go home one more time this coming weekend to make sure I had household money for the next week too. He would pick me up Friday afternoon, and I would ride home with him. Whatever I had spent in the past week, he would then reimburse me as household money. ('Say thank you first, of course, don't forget, you ungrateful bitch...') I carefully examined the receipts I had picked up. I put the one with the largest amount on it in my purse, which only held the two cents I had received in change.

Friday afternoon, punctually at four o'clock, he was at my door. I had already packed my bag so I didn't have to let him into my room.

'Bye,' Fenna shouted at me in the corridor. 'Have a nice weekend!'

Stupid chick, I thought. 'Um yes, you, too.'

'Nice girl,' he said.

When I got home, my mother was elated to see me. She immediately put me at the kitchen table with a big piece of home-baked apple pie. I tried to eat neatly but devoured it like a hungry wolf. She was a wonderful cook, and I was hungry; famished in fact. Cozily, we chatted about this and that, while I ate the second piece of pie she had put on my plate – more slowly this time. As usual, I eyed her and she me, without openly asking how things were going. That wasn't necessary. We just knew, without words being wasted on the subject.

I also did justice to dinner and all the other meals that weekend. My mother was delighted that I liked everything, and she put a number of trays and packets of food ready in the fridge, which I would get with me in the bag with clean laundry on Monday morning. Without him, we had a good time, and we both tried to avoid him as much as possible.

But on Sunday evening we had to 'settle up'. I had to ask for the household money myself. Sufficiently humble, of course.

'Do you have the receipts?' he asked.

I only had the one and I gave it to him. Standing at his desk, I had to wait for him to thoroughly check everything.

He peered at the receipt for a while, then opened his eyes in surprise. 'Nappies?' he asked, shoving the receipt accusingly under my nose, pointing at something.

Indeed, the name of a well-known brand was on the receipt. My heart skipped a beat. I had only looked at the total amount and had not seen that Jac Hermans' supermarket had revamped the till system. The receipt was itemized, and it showed not only amounts but also what had been bought.

Rushing to think of an excuse, I said, 'Er, yes. I'm sure that's a mistake; that must be the sanitary pads I bought. Those new receipts aren't always correct yet.' With that, I trumped him sufficiently, as he was as squeamish as anything. Sanitary pads and menstruation horrified him, and he turned a deep red.

But he recovered quickly. With a grand gesture, he handed me my household money. He also rounded up the amount on the receipt by a quarter.

'Thank you,' I said humbly. Thankfully, humbly enough this time, he didn't want a kiss too.

I quickly put the money in my purse. In my mind I did the math. Would it be enough to pay for my food for a week? Probably, with all the food my mother had waiting for me in the fridge.

I had already put a tube of toothpaste, a bottle of shampoo, and a roll of toilet paper in my bag from the pantry. My mother had caught me at it and had said nothing. She had just given me a look of understanding, while also handing me a jar of applesauce and a tin of peas.

Monday morning at seven o'clock, with a well-filled bag and enough money in my purse, I joined him in the car back to Amsterdam. He always contrived to give me a lift on his way to one of his customers. Not because this was convenient for him, or because he really had to go to that customer urgently, but because it saved the price of a train ticket. After all, he could claim for reimbursement of travel expenses to his customer.

There was no talking along the way. Not by me, because I was afraid of saying the wrong thing. Nor by him, because... well, I don't really know why not.

Arriving at the student flat where I lived, he wanted to walk inside with me, but I narrowly avoided that. 'Sorry, but I have a lecture at nine, so I have to leave right away.' Giving me a penetrating, taunted look, he said goodbye, got into his car and left.

With a thud, I fell on my bed. What a wonderful feeling it was to be alone, with a big bag full of food with me, enough money in my purse for the first couple of days, and a job with my own income in the offing. Lying on my bed, I ate the leftover apple pie my mother had given me, straight out of the foil she had wrapped it in, and without a fork. Then I licked my fingers and took a wonderful nap under the covers. I didn't have a lecture until eleven o'clock.

The next weekend I did not go home. ('Heavens, what has that child of yours come up with now? She'll find out soon enough that she needs to come home when she needs money again,' I heard from my mother later.)

The following Monday afternoon, I cycled to Overtoom, where the Municipal Insurance Department had its offices. At the typing pool, I typed notes in which the department indicated whether someone could claim compensation for damage or not. Damages were usually the result of burglaries in the large housing estates in the Southeastern Bijlmer suburb of the city. It was boring work really, but not tiring, and in a wonderfully heated room where the coffee and tea were free and good.

And financially I had my independence. I counted on him not daring to stop paying the rent for my room (he always paid it directly). He was a terrible miser, but no one was allowed to know.

October 1963 - Household money

From her very first day as a married woman, Mum received household money from him. Although she was a working woman who earned her own income, except for a few years when she had babies, she had to wait for him to hand her the household money every Saturday morning. Her children, when they were old enough, were expected to obediently watch from a distance so that they would learn how to handle money.

Married women in the Netherlands were no longer legally incompetent since 1956, but they still were by the prevailing mores. During the first years of their marriage, she had to hand her salary, which was then still paid in cash in a pay bag, over to him on Friday evenings.

She never had her own bank account during her entire marriage.

Mum didn't agree with all this, but she didn't want to argue with him about it either. However, it was going too far for her to keep a household account book so that everything she spent could be monitored by him.

There were never words wasted on this. As punishment, he simply gave her too little money to run the household. Nothing was ever said about that either. Apparently, he was convinced for a long time that, soon enough, she would come to her senses and would have to show him all her expenses before he would give her even one cent extra. But she never did.

If necessary, she just ate sugar on her toast to make ends meet (he got the last bit of sausage, of course), and every now and then she stole some change from his wallet when he was in the shower. Not all of it at once, of course, but just so much that it wouldn't be noticed. Her little son, who caught her doing this once, immediately demanded two quarters for himself to buy an ice cream.

When her daughter moved to Amsterdam, he shifted his tactics to her. Back then, there were no scholarships that were independent of parents' income, so it was soon clear that she was the next in line to ask him humbly for household money. It was for her own good, according to him.

Every weekend, she was expected to come home and show her supermarket receipts to him. Living expenses incurred were offset against a sparingly allocated advance. Of course, by living expenses he meant only food and drink. He paid textbooks and rent directly to the bookshop and the landlord. And he counted on Mum to buy clothes for her daughter from time to time. Expenses to participate in student life were not eligible for reimbursement, he had sternly stated. Imagine HIS daughter at bawdy student parties! That would only delay studies and 'God knows what other dangers' these parties would lead to (he was not religious). No matter how much she pleaded with him, he stuck to his position.

But she wouldn't have been a good daughter to her mother if she hadn't found a solution. After each errand to the supermarket, she simply picked up a receipt from the floor in the shop that had a few guilders more on it than her own. And she gave that to him instead. This left her with some money to participate in student life, albeit on a very modest scale.

She was forbidden a part-time job. Only studying was allowed, so that she would graduate in the nominal time of statistically four years he said it would take. According to him, he knew exactly about the statistics on the length of study time – as well as every other possible statistic, for that matter.

All in all, daughter dearest was able to just make ends meet without having to turn down invitations to parties all the time. She was also able to invite someone for dinner every now and then, and she was able to bring a present to a birthday party once that was not food. She also managed to hide her embarrassment about her expense practices from her fellow students.

12 February, 1986 – Luck

I had finished my first working days, and I was proud; immensely proud of my achievement. I had pulled it off. Just a little longer and then I would get my first salary. It was a wonderful feeling.

On workdays, I sat upright at the typewriter, took a sheet of data from the left-hand tray marked 'in', typed out a note according to the instructions on a large poster on the wall, and then put it, together with the sheet from the left-hand box, into the right-hand box marked 'out'. It wasn't difficult, and I could observe my colleagues well while working.

Everyone was friendly there, I soon realized. There was a cheerful atmosphere with Freek (floppy ears and the flattest Amsterdam accent I had ever heard), Jolanda (the biggest Ajax fan I ever knew), Marco (always smiling), and Edgar (my boss).

Often, there was also cake from someone, treated in honor of their birthday, because Ajax had won a match, or because eating cake was simply something we all craved. In short, I had a great time there.

From the conversations I had, I understood that I owed my job to Diny, a colleague who had gone on maternity leave. Actually, they had hired me as a temp for just a few months.

But after only two days of my working there, they heard that Diny was planning to stop coming altogether. She wanted to stay home with her baby. And no matter how much they urged her, she stuck to her decision. Eventually, she didn't even pick up the phone anymore. Her former colleagues couldn't understand a thing of what was going on.

I didn't understand either. In fact, I thought she was unemancipated. Surely you could work if you had a child? There were such things as crèches, or maybe there were babysitters on offer, too! I didn't really want to understand. But as long as I could hold my job, it was fine with me.

Edgar had asked me that morning if I wanted to stay a little longer. Well, gladly. Now I had to see him less often; preferably never again. But it did gnaw at me that I wouldn't see my mother as often either.

8 November, 1963 – Connections are cut

In 1963, the distribution of natural gas from Slochteren had begun, and the State Treasury was slowly filling up. There was soon a tightening in the Dutch labor market, but the tradition that had started just after the war, to build a better life somewhere far away in a foreign country, had not yet disappeared in the early 1960s. Indeed, young couples were encouraged by the government to emigrate.

Emigration was a very big step at the time. Information about the destination country was scarce and mainly disseminated through cozy information evenings for newlyweds. They received the flawed information through recruiting posters and leaflets printed in dribs and drabs with stencil machines. Many left for Canada. But Australia was also in demand.

The information evenings were organized by embassy staff of that country, in cooperation with officials from the Dutch Ministry of Foreign Affairs. Sometimes Foreign Minister Mr. Luns allowed officials of the Minister of Social Work Ms. (!) Schouwenaar-Franssen to also contribute to the information evenings.

The great financial benefits of emigration were emphasized, especially for those who had the right professions. And that's what these newlyweds had. He was a metal worker, and Mum was a nurse. In short, they got themselves signed up for the long boat trip to Australia, even though they didn't speak English at all and only knew that life was good there, that driving was on the wrong side of the road, that the weather would be hot, and that there would be kangaroos.

In retrospect, they considered themselves very naïve that they had left for the other side of the world virtually unprepared, although he never openly admitted this. But Mum did.

On 8 November, 1963, his eldest brother took them to Rotterdam, from where they would be taken to Australia aboard the *Aurelia* in six weeks. Grandpa and Grandma had also come along for the occasion. The closer they got to Rotterdam, the quieter everyone became.

On the quay, it was a chaotic mob of emigrants who gave a last quick hug to their relatives, whom they would leave behind in the freezing cold. There was a lot of crying, though everyone tried to pretend it was a party by throwing serpentines and waving big, white handkerchiefs a lot. The ship's horn was deafening when the mooring lines were cast off, and it also lasted for a long time. Grandma cried and moaned: 'I'll never see him again.' But hardly anyone heard that, with all the noise.

That she would never see her son again was not such a crazy thought. There was no intercontinental air travel then, and flying was prohibitively expensive anyway. A boat trip took six weeks one way and was free for emigrants only under certain conditions. Family visits were therefore not possible. Telephoning was an unheard-of luxury and near impossible to someone abroad. And the post took six weeks, unless you used an airmail letter; then it took two weeks, and if you were lucky, one week. But that again was much more expensive than a regular letter. In short, saying goodbye on the quay in Rotterdam was basically final. But oh, the better life beckoned.

For Mum, it meant that she could continue working. In the Netherlands, she had been sacked immediately after her wedding day. This was a common practice at the time, anchoring most married women inexorably to their kitchen counters. But in Australia, it was perfectly normal, even a requirement, for her to work. And for him, the better life he longed for meant above all: property. He dreamt of his own house and a car, things that seemed unattainable to him in the Netherlands.

It was a pity that they did not have a private cabin of their own on board the ship, though, he thought. Men and women slept separately on board. The *Aurelia* – formerly a ship for the military – only had multi-person cabins with bunk beds; dormitories, in fact. Dormitories for men, and dormitories for women and children.

Mum didn't mind so much. She thought sex was a messy business anyway, and she had more cause to chatter with the other women on board than with her brand-new husband. She thoroughly enjoyed the voyage and the rare trips to foreign quays where the ship docked on its way to Melbourne. For instance, she saw Naples and Aden. Later, she always proudly showed the pictures in her photo album to her children.

There was no television on board, and only when the boat docked could the (local) radio be listened to. The passengers entertained themselves with simple games on deck, singing, crafts, and one hour a day of English lessons. Upon crossing the equator, there was a solemn ceremony with a crew member dressed as Neptune, and everyone was given a glass of champagne and a certificate signed by the captain. It was as if the passengers on the ship were teleported to the other side of the world in a communal, safe cocoon.

After the boat trip, Mum managed to speak a few words of poor English, but reading was still difficult. Only when they had been in the Bonegilla migrant camp for a few days, and after much toil with a borrowed dictionary, could she understand what was in the English newspaper in which they had packed a souvenir for her in Aden, and which she had kept to learn English words from:

'KENNEDY IS KILLED BY SNIPER AS HE RIDES
IN CAR IN DALLAS. JOHNSON SWORN IN ON PLANE'

read the front page of *The New York Times* of 23 November, 1963. She was stunned by the then ancient news.

She didn't get much time to think about it, though. She had to work in the camp kitchen, otherwise they wouldn't get out on time and they couldn't get a good job. They had to show to camp management that they really wanted to work, then they would have the best jobs to choose from, according to him. And the fact that she earned some pocket money by working in the camp kitchen, that was a nice bonus. For him, that is.

14 February, 1986 – Caught

I saw him sitting in the kitchen. He had been let in by Fenna. And she was enjoying tea with him. They were having a good time together, you could tell. She undoubtedly liked him a lot and never missed an opportunity to bend down so he could look deep into her cleavage. As she walked away, his cheeky gaze slid seductively over her tight buttocks. Cold shivers ran down my spine. And I couldn't manage to work him out the door without him first making a visit to my room, where he questioned me about her.

Secretly, I rubbed my aching ribs once in a while and tried to concentrate on his questions, so that I could keep answering them properly. It was a huge relief when, after half an hour, he got up and left.

I had never really liked Fenna. In fact, I thought she was a vulgar slut. She was man-crazy and only too happy to parade around with a new 'sugar daddy' every time. She would brag about it in our communal kitchen and show off the presents she had received. Often it was jewelry, which she sold in the pawnshop on Haarlemmerdijk.

She didn't study; she was enrolled as a student more for form's sake and let herself be maintained by all the guys she could seduce with her twisting ass. And if she was horny or drunk (or both) and there was no other guy around, she'd do it with Wieger.

She was careful not to get pregnant or contract an STD. In the kitchen, she proudly explained which contraceptive pill she experienced the horrific side effects from, which sex toys she had, and which size condoms and lubricants she kept in her bedside table and her handbag.

25 December, 1965 – Christmas baby

Before the introduction of birth control pills, women had to be damned careful not to get pregnant after sex, even if they were married. After all, a child was not always wanted and often came too early, even before a suitable house and sufficient savings had been accumulated by the parents to raise a family without too much worry.

But he found fucking a fine activity which should preferably take place daily. Although he had told Mum not to get pregnant, as a non-believer he regularly reminded her of her Catholic marital obligations. An impossible combination, therefore, of an injunction both for and against the acts performed in the marital bed. And despite the Catholic Church's objections, after a few weeks of persistent bickering and harassment, Mum decided to proceed with periodic abstinence.

To keep track of when her fertile (and therefore sexless) days would be, she had to record when she menstruated in a kind of mechanical calculator and regularly take her temperature. She could record this data in the plastic cylinder with small rotating discs. The top disc would then indicate on which days of the month there was a risk of pregnancy. Using the device, periodic abstinence would be much safer than without it.

She explained to him how it all worked. He only half listened, because everything to do with his wife's body and how it worked, he found embarrassing. Only in bed – in the dark and neatly under the blankets – did he like to use it, gladly and often. He did understand that there were some days in the month when he wouldn't get his way, but really thinking about it, he didn't want to then. Soon Mum was pregnant, and gave birth to a son.

A son, yes, he was still proud of that, but changing nappies? He would not do it. Not even when Mum had to work at night and he was sulking in bed alone. He stuffed cotton wool into his ears in an effort not to hear the screeching. The nappy rash he most certainly didn't want to hear about; that was not his cup of tea. And after the first few months of his life, the child never cried again.

Soon, Mum was pregnant again. At the GP's surgery (her son – the earlier accident – was crowing with joy on her arm), she burst into tears. When the doctor asked what the problem was, the story of the lonely immigrant with a potentate as a husband in the foreign country on the other side of the world came out in fits and starts. Astonished, her little son poked at her tears with a chubby little finger.

The doctor looked indignant. 'You didn't put it in there!' he roared across the consulting room, as he too poked a chubby little finger, but this time at Mum's bulging belly.

Over four months later, and all on her own, she gave birth to her daughter in the Port Augusta Maternity Hospital. The staff were busy with the communal Christmas barbecue, sitting in the courtyard enjoying the beautiful summer weather. No matter how much she had called out, no one had come to help her. When, after an hour, someone finally came to check on her, the woman cut the umbilical cord without further ado. She also immediately washed mother and daughter completely clean, ashamed that she had not been there sooner.

The baby was then taken away by the nurse and placed in a cot in the nursery room, although Mum would have preferred to keep her in bed with her. Just like earlier with her infant son, she was immediately besotted with her baby.

He was not. When he appeared at his wife's bedside hours later, he had only one question for her: 'You do know whose fault it is, don't you, that we have this child?'

She knew that all too well, but she didn't say so.

There was a card waiting for him on the bedside table with the name of his daughter on it. The card was meant to be shown through the glass of the nursery room to the nurse, who would then pick out the right baby for him from one of the cots.

He did not use it and only saw his daughter three days later, when his wife – with her baby daughter in her arms – was allowed to go home to the suburb of Port

Augusta where they lived. She plodded on, trying to make the best of things with her children.

She didn't have much fun with him, but at some point she spoke English quite well, so she chatted with the neighbor. The latter took care of her, almost like a welfare project. The woman and her eldest daughter, Annie, took turns babysitting the children, and Mum went out to work in a local mental institution. He was fine with that, as her income far exceeded what she paid to the girl next door for her babysitting services.

Once back home in the Netherlands, Mum had to stop working. Women belong at home with the children – that's how everyone in the Netherlands thought about it at the time, and so did he. Nor did he want his family to know that Mum had done paid work in faraway Australia. The story he spun was that the children – little accidents – had thrown a spanner in the works, and that was why they had returned to the Netherlands. Otherwise, they would have stayed there.

'Stop it!' called Grandma. 'They are beautiful children, and at least now I can see them. They are no accidents. Look at those sweet faces.' The little boy she loved unconditionally because he was a boy. The girl she thought was special because she was a girl (she herself had given birth to five sons and not a single girl), and perhaps also because she was a Christmas baby.

18 April, 1986 – The sweetest daddy in the entire world

On my way to work, I read a newspaper someone had left on the tram. Rebels in Sudan had downed a plane, Reagan threatened a veto (no idea what for), and Prince was performing in Ahoy. It all interested me very little, nothing really. In all honesty, I must confess that I rarely read a newspaper. And I never watched the news on television at all. I didn't even have a television, by the way.

I flicked through the newspaper and read something here and there, which I couldn't remember. On page 5, there was an article about the British secret service, which was supposedly in need of reform. Pffff, nice and important.

I stared blankly outside. People were just going to work or to the shops, signboards and shop windows also looked unsurprising, cyclists were ignoring red lights. In short: nothing out of the ordinary.

The newspaper rustled as I crossed my legs and glanced at it again. The family reports testified of beloved dead who were missed by their relatives. One notice was about a father who had died young and who was remembered by his children as 'the sweetest daddy in the whole world'. Nothing else with great news value.

I always liked the classified ads. People were looking for mates, and dogs and cats were looking for new owners. I imagined the women would be paired with cuddly cats, and the men accidentally with nasty fighting dogs that should have been put down years ago. A grin must have appeared on my face, because the woman opposite me on the tram smiled kindly and asked me if I had read something nice in the paper.

September 1968 – Our Father

In the village there was only one small kindergarten, and it was Roman Catholic. Because he was an atheist and had difficulty with Mum's Catholic background, a non-denominational kindergarten had to be looked for outside the village. Not far away was a good school that boasted that royal princes and princesses had learned to paste and cut there. An excellent choice for their own children, they thought in rare agreement.

As the exclusivity of the school was further underlined by a school bus which stopped every morning at the street corner, they were very proud about their choice. Early in the morning, the children were dropped off at the bus stop. Mum, and all the other mothers who walked to the bus stop, were eventually practiced in casting pitying glances twice daily towards the mothers who brought their children on foot to and from the backward Catholic school.

Throughout the day, the toddlers were entertained at an excellent degree of sophistication. And after lunch, of course, they had to nap on specially provided stretchers. In the mornings, they often did pasting, cutting, and finger-painting projects. And every afternoon, educationally sound lessons had to be learnt. Like the lesson that you could only yawn with your hand in front of your mouth.

The little boy, who was already in the second kindergarten class, apparently did not know this lesson very well. One day, he came into his sister's classroom looking bedraggled, accompanied by a classmate. There were letters written on his forehead. Mum later said it read, 'This little boy yawned without his hand in front of his mouth. Sign here.' Miss Greet had marked something on the boy's forehead with her ballpoint pen. Amazed, his sister sat on her chair; she didn't understand a thing. But the fact that it was not a fun game her brother had to take part in, was clear.

On the school bus home, brother and sister sat hand-in-hand. He still looked sad and said nothing. His forehead looked a little red and rough, but the ink was gone. Already at the bus stop, mum unraveled by bits and pieces what had happened that day.

Indignant, she dragged her offspring home. Surprised, they heard her excitedly talking on the phone to one of their teachers. Angry words rolled out of her mouth, and a little spit bubble formed at the corner of her lips. The longer the phone call went on, the prouder the children felt. Phew, nice!

'You'll never go there again,' Mum shouted, after swatting the handset on the hook with a spiteful gesture. 'No more crying now. Mummy will make it all right,' she said, stroking her son's head. But the boy had not cried yet, so he didn't have to stop. Her little daughter did cry, but with relief.

The boy went to the local primary school almost immediately. But the girl had to go through another year of kindergarten. That was now allowed with the Roman Catholics, and she loved it there. The teacher was sweet and told wonderful stories about Our Father. She also taught her a kind of verse about that Father that she had to recite with her eyes closed and her hands neatly folded. She especially loved the first line. In the evening at dinner, she asked her mother, 'Mummy, when is our daddy going to heaven?'

May 1986 – Family weekend

The combination of family and holiday homes: it's really never been my cup of tea. So, the idea that my grandparents were going to organize a family weekend in a bungalow park with their five sons and entourage, was reason enough for me to search diligently for a good reason not to join them.

At that time, I had been living in a student flat in Amsterdam for almost a year and a half, studying at the University of Amsterdam. I was expected to come home every weekend and collect the household money for the following week. On Friday afternoons, he would pick me up in person; he always 'happened to be in the neighborhood' to provide a customer with a new supply of curtain rails.

We never made an appointment for the rides home, yet every Friday he showed up at my door. In short, it seemed like I was pretty much in the pincer; if I didn't go home, I would be out of money and even have to scrounge food from housemates in the student flat. And they weren't very generous with it. They thought I was just a provincial bitch with antics. I didn't want to smoke pot with them, for instance.

According to Wieger, I 'had to get a good fuck and then my tomfoolery would be over,' or a variation on that same theme, which he repeated with great certainty (anger almost) all the time. And then everyone would roll about with laughter. I stayed as far away from them as possible. So, all in all, I was often hungry and at unseen moments I would sometimes steal something edible form someone else's kitchen cupboard.

My visit to the temp agency had landed me a part-time job at the Municipal Insurance Department. For several weeks I had been commuting back and forth between my lectures in the city center and Overtoom, where the service was housed. I studied and earned a nice sum of money, and I soon calculated that I could survive four to eight weeks without having to go home.

Buying food was now no longer a problem. So it was with some confidence that I told him I wouldn't be able to come home for the next four weeks, which also included the family weekend. I said I was too busy studying. It seemed like an excellent excuse to me, especially since he always told me that I should graduate in the 'statistical average, nominal length of study' of four years.

But he didn't agree. According to him, I could bring some of my textbooks and do some studying every now and then over the weekend, so I could still join the fun. After a brief telephone consultation with my mother, I decided not to budge.

So, I took more drastic measures and stayed out later and later on Friday nights, forcing him to wait for me for hours at the door of my student flat. I would sit in the university library to study, surrounded by books that were, of course, indispensable in the process. When I got home by dark, I hoped he'd given up and left. After the third week, that was indeed the case. He stayed away the fourth week, too. I was ecstatic and felt I had beat him! At least that's how it seemed.

But of course, I was wrong. At the request of my grandparents, he had taken on the organization of the family weekend and booked the holiday homes. He was considered an expert in the family when it came to holiday homes. After all, he had several of his own.

It should have been no surprise that the holiday park happened to be fully booked during the planned weekend, and there was a delay for a week. I knew nothing about this. So, when he showed up at my door again a week later, I unsuspectingly got into his car. I wanted to see my mother again. It didn't bother me that he didn't speak a word to me the whole drive as punishment. All was nice and quiet.

Like a frightened little bird, my mother was waiting for us in the kitchen. 'Have you spoken to Dad yet?' she asked me, shoving two packed bags towards the door. 'We have to leave immediately, otherwise we will be late.'

My household money, of course, he only settled with me for the previous week. He never asked me how I had made ends meet during the other three weeks.

In the weeks that followed, when the sharp edge on one of my front teeth started to bother me more and more, I didn't have money to go to the dentist. Fortunately, it was only a tiny bit that had broken off. Eventually, the sharp edge dulled on its own. Until I was twenty-five, I never went to the dentist except once.

June 1974 – Holiday home

He was almost always late for dinner or 'the hot meal', as they called it back then. No matter how long Mum waited with the food on the stove, at some point she and her children had to start eating, especially if it was a school day the next day. Often, therefore, they were already eating when he came in and joined them without too much ceremony. Usually, he was quite cranky by then. It was rarely cozy when the four of them were sitting at the table.

One day he came home again while they were already eating spinach. From the doorway, taking off his coat, he called cheerfully, 'Hello there!'

In terror, the girl choked on the last bite of spinach. Her little brother, normally a chatterbox, was dumbfounded, and Mum's hand stuck somewhere between her plate and her mouth. Slowly, the green goo dripped off her fork.

In the deep silence, interrupted only by stuffy coughing, he said, 'Today is a big day for us. I have bought a holiday home!'

Mum's fork clattered onto her plate. Blearily, she asked, 'What do you mean?'

The children looked at each other in amazement. 'Holiday,' the girl gurgled. It sounded exciting. They would go on holiday! She had to tell everyone at school the next morning.

'Daddy, where exactly is this holiday home?' the boy asked.

'Close to Grandma's,' he said, already stuffing big bites of spinach into his mouth.

'Don't spill your food, darling,' Mum said to the little boy. 'And when you've finished your plates, leave the table so I can talk to Dad.'

The girl immediately slid off her chair. Her relief that she could leave the table was greater than her sadness over the missed dessert, about which Mum had said nothing.

Late into the night, she heard her parents talking to each other in a loud tone. Every now and then she would catch a word: money, house, why, consultation...

Early the next weekend, the whole family was in the car heading for the holiday home. In the children's dreams it had become a sun-drenched Cinderella castle, and they could hardly wait to get there.

'Look, this is where Daddy was born,' he said at the bend in the road where he always said this. The boy rolled his eyes, but otherwise there was silence in the car.

After the next bend, he turned right. They followed a forest path, and at a muddy patch he stopped the car. Through the trees they could just make out a small, dilapidated shack. 'We're here,' he called, got out and stretched. Stunned, the rest of the family sat looking around.

The children smiled broadly at each other. He was joking. Nice, he almost never did. When they saw Mum's face, however, they knew he was dead serious. For a moment, they were disappointed. But they cheered up quickly, thinking about playing together in the forest.

From the look of her, Mum was not best pleased. 'How did you plan on having holidays here?' she asked.

'Easy,' he said. 'The kids will have fun, and now I'd like a beer.'

'But that roof must be as leaky as a basket. Look at all that moss and those sagging gutters!'

'Well, we'll do something about it if and when it's convenient. It's not raining now.'

He put the key in the lock and with a grand gesture swung the door open, which let out a wretched moan. Inside, it stank of mold and clogged drains. And it was small; ridiculously small.

'Yuck,' said the little boy, holding his nose and pointing at the large black spider hanging in an impressive web above the window.

'Ah, it won't do anything,' he said. He took off his shoe and hit the spider with it. *Splat!*

In the years that followed, the roof was repaired, the floors tiled, the drains unblocked, the kitchen whitewashed, and the cold hutch that was supposed to pass for a bathroom cleaned up. All with the combined efforts of parents and children. Children's hands turned out to be good at grouting tiles, he soon discovered. And children were also good at scrubbing. Nice and free, too, even if the orders to work had to be reinforced every now and then with a hefty slap on the buttocks or a twist of an ear here and there. That gave him a taste for more holiday homes...

Holidaying as other people did was out of the question. Every weekend, something had to be done in order for the holiday home to be ready in time for the next guests who were willing to pay money to rent his shack. The children never played in the woods, and they never spent a single holiday in it.

But they did have a leaky tent trailer. It was an Alpenkreuzer, with which they went to almost free nature campsites – without hot showers – in Germany every year for a week.

'*Ganz billig*,' he would shout on the way there.

The children liked it a lot, playing in the mud. And they also didn't mind skipping the shower for a day or so if the water was really too cold.

Because the boy was a tough daredevil who always protected the girl, she happily and blindly followed him through the worst dirt. But Mum was exasperated with all the filth she was expected to clean up during these camping expeditions. All day she was busy cleaning, scrubbing, and washing as best she could with cold water from a small basin. And cooking on a gas burner flickering in the wind was no fun for her either.

22 August, 1986 – Bad luck

Last week, I had managed to avoid him again, so I had a whole weekend of freedom ahead of me. It was a warm, almost hot Friday night in the summer of my second year as a student in Amsterdam, and I was trying to find some coolness in the open window of my dorm room. I had opened the windows and was sitting on the windowsill with my legs out, drinking a glass of ice-cold buttermilk. Too bad, though, that my brother and his girlfriend Annet had left for France on his motorcycle. Would I have enough money to go to the cinema? They had wonderful air conditioning there. Carefully, I got up from the windowsill and went to find my bag. But my purse wasn't in it. Where had I put the thing? After some rummaging in the cupboard, I found it in my coat pocket.

At that moment, there was a knock on my door. I stood motionless and listened carefully to hear who was there. Nothing was said. But there was another knock on the door, louder this time. Silently, I crept towards the door. Holding my breath, I looked through the peephole. Yes, there he was. My hand went for the bolt on the door to let him in, but just in time I changed my mind. I took a step back and waited for what was to come.

Hard banging this time. He didn't just give up easily, of course. 'I know you're home, Kiki. Open this door immediately, you silly cow!'

My heart was pounding in my throat, but I didn't. After a few minutes, I heard him walking away. Somewhere down the corridor, I heard him talking animatedly to someone. Listening again carefully, I heard it was to Fenna.

Cautiously, I set my door ajar and looked down the corridor. Fenna was just waving him off after giving him a kiss on the cheek. He reciprocated with a slap on her ass. I was surprised she allowed it, but she seemed unaware of any danger. Yes, they liked each other very much.

But now he was at my door again. This time I was just not quick enough, and before I knew it, he walked into my room. He pulled the door shut behind him. Gosh.

There he was, standing in the middle of my room. 'I just want to talk to you about last week,' he said, looking me up and down. 'Why didn't you open your door for me?

Tell me that first. Don't you owe me a little respect and gratitude?'

He was getting closer and closer, and I kept stepping back, trying to stay out of reach of his hands and feet. But when my back was literally against the wall, there was nothing I could do but wait for what was to come. I broke into a sweat and I tried to avoid his gaze. A first tap landed on my cheek.

Swiftly, he then grabbed me by my throat and banged my head against the wall. 'I always do everything I possibly can, often at the expense of myself. And all I get in return is your sour face all the time. Do you actually realize how much I love you?'

I tried to pull his hand away, but it only squeezed my throat harder.

'Surely, I'm only doing everything for your own good! Why don't you just come home like your mum and I expect? She's crying her eyes out over you and your ungrateful conduct. It's so bad that she can't even cook for me every now and then. Do you have a boyfriend, maybe, making you think you don't need me anymore, who you let pay everything for you, in return for letting him touch your breasts?'

His free hand grabbed my left breast. 'Or are you just a big slut who lets herself be groped by any random student who pays for her food and drink after a lovemaking session? WELL?!' He tugged at my blouse, hard. 'With those whore clothes of yours, of course all the guys will be following you like you've got molasses on your ass.'

He wanted to move his hand from my chest to my crotch, but I was struggling too much for that. With both hands, he squeezed my throat. The back of my head was pressed flat against the wall. His face was very close, but I could hardly see it any more among all the white, red, and green dots splattered somewhere before my eyes.

My arms got heavier and I was hanging against the wall. I couldn't get air into my lungs anymore and couldn't get it out either. Fear seemed to give way to a kind of ecstasy. It was somehow not unpleasant.

But no, wait a minute. A last vestige of anger swept through my entire body, and I just barely managed to deliver a hefty kick. With an exasperated cry, he let go. 'Damn it, YOU SHOULD NEVER HAVE BEEN BORN!' he hissed. I fell on the ground and could only greedily gasp for air. Out of the corner of my eye, I saw him lashing out with his leg. The first kick landed on my hip. My brain registered it, but I felt nothing.

The second kick stopped mid-air, following a knock on my door, and Wieger's voice calling out, 'Hey, you bitch, can you fuck a little quieter? I can't study with that noise, and I have an exam tomorrow. If you don't shut it, I'll call the caretaker!'

Startled, he stood in the middle of my room. I was still panting hard, trying to fill my lungs with as much oxygen as possible.

'Yes, let's have a little less of that panting, too, you dirty slut,' Wieger called out. And he drummed hard and long on the door with his fists.

He only had eyes for the door, as if Wieger would step through it. But the latter apparently thought it was enough after a few minutes and walked away. Wieger's brogues clicked on the linoleum in the corridor, heading towards his room.

He listened tensely, waited a for a few more seconds and then left my room. Not once had he looked back at me.

December 1970 – Not nice

It was a dreary day in late December, just after Christmas, the little girl's birthday. In honor of the big day which she had been looking forward to for weeks, all the preschoolers from the apartment building had come to her house. Together they had drunk lemonade, eaten cake, listened in a large circle to a fairy tale read by Mum from a large library book, and (the ultimate joy!) unwrapped presents.

From the neighboring children she got a roll of sticky gumballs, a little doll with real clothes on, and a beautiful birthday card with a picture of a clown on it. But the biggest and most exciting gift was a sled. He had given it to her, just as the other children were being picked up by their mothers, allowing for them to witness his generosity.

The sled was clearly not new, but a desirable gift that she could hardly take her eyes and hands off. It made her feel wonderfully happy!

The sled had to be tried, preferably right away. But it was already getting dark by then, so she had to be patient until tomorrow, Mummy had said.

Excitedly, she and her older brother had been dribbling by the front door since the first light of dawn. The toddlers could barely stand still as Mummy wrapped them up properly against the cold. She was always very 'wrapping-crazy' and the same today, as scarves, hats, and thick mittens came into play. But something exciting was waiting for them, so it had to be done.

'Come on. Those kids have been waiting so long already.'

The only answer she got was a deep sigh from the back room, where he lay in the double bed. But he didn't get out of bed, just turned over once more.

'Come on,' Mum tried again after fifteen minutes, nodding encouragingly at her little daughter. Nervously, her brother hopped from one foot to the other.

After another deep sigh, he appeared in the doorway with a sleepy head. Seeing that everyone was ready at the door, he turned around and agonizingly slowly put on his clothes. The cup of tea that Mum had put wordlessly on his bedside table, he drank in small sips.

'*Okay* then, hmmmmm,' he said, and finally put on his coat at the door. He then took his daughter on his left arm and grabbed the sled with his right hand. With his little son at his heels, he stumbled down the three flights of stairs.

'Have fun, darlings,' Mum sang through the stairwell.

Outside the door of the apartment building, there was a thin layer of snow, through which the neighborhood children were traipsing. Carefully looking left and right, they slid across the street, where there was a large lawn with snow that still looked pristine. After all, crossing the road yourself was forbidden for small children. And in those days, when parental authority was still such that children did what parents commanded, the neighborhood children had looked longingly at the lawn across the street but had not set foot on it.

Standing in the white plain, he threw down the sled and commanded the boy to sit on it. Then he put the girl on the back. The party was about to start. After another deep sigh, he picked up the rope and began pulling the sled. With the thin layer of snow, this turned out to be not so easy. The irons kept hitting the ground or the grass under the snow, but the kids didn't care. They were thoroughly enjoying themselves. He clearly found it less amusing.

'GGGGDDDDMMMN IT,' he mumbled every time the sled stalled again for a moment.

After about five minutes, he had had enough. The sled had come to a halt on a patch of grass under the big tree, where the snow had been unable to reach. With a firm tug and the utterance of an expletive, he pulled the sled free again, and at the same time the girl lay on her back in the snow behind the sled.

'Daddy,' she sniffled, horrified as she saw her brother's back disappear from her field of vision.

'Oh, my darling girl,' he said, when he saw that she had fallen. 'Get up.'

When she didn't get up immediately because her thick winter coat got in her way, he walked back, annoyed, put her clumsily back on her short legs, and patted her back to get rid of the clumps of snow that were stuck to it.

By her hand, he led her towards the sled and pulled her up over the seat. There he released her hand, and with a thud she was back on the sled. He then took the rope and again started pulling it. After a few moments there was another tug on the rope, even though they were now sliding in the middle of a beautiful white stretch. And *hop*, there she was floundering again, only to be put back on the sled forcibly. Her little brother sat rigid on the sled and clung to it with all his might. Not once did he dare look back at his sister.

This strange ritual repeated itself about six times. The last time, as the girl lay cold, wet, and covered in snot on the ground, she suddenly saw him hovering above her. He had a strange expression on his face.

'Come on, dear,' he said with thin lips, and he looked out of the corner of his eyes to the balcony of their flat, where

Mum was watching the scene with her hands cupped in front of her mouth.

Smiling sarcastically, he pulled the girl upright.

'Daddy isn't nice,' she cried.

'Are you saying I am not nice, sweetheart?' he asked, clasping her arm just a tad tighter and pulling it up so far that she was dangling by her arm in the air again.

She kicked at his shins as hard as she could and fell to the ground. Screaming, she scrambled up and ran towards the flat. Without looking left or right, she crossed the street and stumbled up the three flights of stairs to Mum, who lovingly welcomed her with a hug and a mug of hot chocolate. Her brother sat on the sled for quite some time that afternoon.

In the evening, the girl was not allowed dessert. He thought that was an appropriate punishment for crossing the street. That was naughty, he said.

The next morning, when he had stepped out the door to go to work, Mum placed a bowl of vanilla custard in front of the girl. 'From last night, honey. Don't tell Daddy, though.'

23 August, 1986 – The letter

From my bed, it felt like a laborious round-the-world trip to the toilet, the sink, and back. Everywhere hurt, both physically and mentally. Self-pity alternated with anger, and these emotions which raced through me, exhausted me. Consequently, I slept a lot and ate only the biscuits that I had in an open roll on my bedside table. I drank water standing at the sink every time I went to the toilet. I didn't dare show up in the kitchen anyway, even if I could have reached it without stumbling ostentatiously.

Thank God it was Saturday and I didn't have to go to work yet. I resolved to get out of bed on Sunday, take a long shower, and eat well. Then Monday I would be back on my feet. Hopefully, by then I would have the energy to change my sheets, because now the bed already smelled sour from my sweat.

He was busy with very different things, as it turned out. He had written his letter to me yesterday. One of my roommates had slipped it under my door.

Apeldoorn, 22 August, 1986

Dear Kiki,

Why can't you ever even consider my feelings. After all, I've always done my best to give you and your brother the life I never had as a child myself. Does it really cost you too much effort to show me a little affection. Or at least some gratitude. Why do you always flinch when I want to put my arm around you or just sit next to you on the couch. Am I a monster to you. And why don't we hear from you more often. Surely, you were just as guilty as me for our argument yesterday. It's a mystery to me why you always portray me as an ogre, while you're always challenging me. Don't you understand that sometimes I have to do things that you don't like, but which are for your own good. Your mother wants nothing more than to hear from you, you know that. You make her miserable, but of course you don't care at all when you are as selfish as you are.

Hopefully, you will be wise. Next Friday I will pick you up and I will take you home. Mum will be very happy to see you again. And despite everything, let me say: no hard feelings!

Your loving father

I read it again.

Such a strange letter. Strangely worded, too, as if he had taken hours to write everything down in such a way that it would be clear to an unsuspecting reader that I was an ungrateful brat. Weird, too, that so many questions were hidden in the text. But wait, not hidden. No, they were just all in there.

Behind each question, I put the missing question mark with a red felt-tip pen. No, that wasn't yet what I wanted. With my ballpoint pen I also wrote the answers to the questions on the paper: *Sure! No way. Just because. Yes. Leave her out of this,* and so on. It was a useless but satisfying chore. Staring at the ceiling, I fantasized about saying everything with dignity and calm straight to his face.

Under his last words, I put my own question: Have you ever really loved anyone?

7 November, 1975 – I love you so much

Friday night, on the way to visit Grandpa and Grandma, he turned on the radio. The radio cassette player was a nice, modern gadget in his latest car. Of course, no one had any say over which cassette tape would be played or which station would be put on, let alone how loud the sound should be. If a cassette was not played because they all had been heard so many times, he usually kept turning the knobs until something about sports came up on the radio. And then he would loudly shout along with the sports reporters. 'GOAL, GOOOOOAAAAAAALL!' The children of course kept their mouths shut, so as not to spoil his fun after a busy working week.

Today, he did not manage to find the right station immediately. Having to keep both hands on the wheel when overtaking, the radio remained tuned to a station with music.

Ramses Shaffy and Liesbeth List sang about love. The girl had heard their song many times over the years, as it was usually (perhaps always) in the charts, but she had never really listened to the lyrics. She only heard the *'I love you so much'* bit loud and clear. And although she didn't understand a thing else about the song, she loved that bit, because it was sung with such passion. And sincerely, too; it wasn't just a few words. However young she was, she understood that there were people somewhere who loved each other unconditionally and wholeheartedly. Really beautiful, it gave her a lump in her throat.

Fortunately, he left the music on. 'And in second place in the top 40 is *Love Hurts* by Nazareth!' the presenter screamed excitedly. And almost immediately that hit song reverberated through the car.

The girl stole a glance at her brother, but he looked out the window unfazed.

Unfortunately, he found it necessary to sing the last verse along loudly and out of tune. Mum looked aside in surprise, as he had suddenly put his hand on her leg. She looked at his hand as if it were a dirty insect she should fight off.

'Um, honey, wouldn't it be better to keep your hands on the wheel?'

Annoyed, he squeezed her leg viciously, then grabbed the steering wheel with both hands again.

26 August, 1986 – Confession

I had hardly slept over the weekend, so looked tired in the mirror over the sink. On my throat this time, a handprint was visible in shades of blue and grey. I hadn't felt like answering questions, so I had called in sick to Edgar yesterday. Since I was quite hoarse, I had mentioned that I had a sore throat. It must have sounded plausible, because he wished me well and said he hoped I would come in the next day, because there was a lot of work and some colleagues were still on holiday.

So today, I did have to go to work. I could not and did not want to call in sick again. As a temp, I did not receive any sick pay, and I desperately needed the money.

I treated myself to my last two paracetamols and then I dressed myself in front of the mirror as best I could, arranging a scarf around my neck to cover the bruises. It had to do, even though the scarf would be far too hot on this beautiful summer day. And I looked frumpy with it, too.

Reluctantly, I hoisted myself up the stairs to the office on Overtoom and managed to walk to my desk. Fortunately, there was no one in yet. With my back to the door, I took a typing job from the tray to the left of my electronic typewriter, inserted a new sheet of stationery, and began working. For an hour I was able to work undisturbed, and slowly the monotonous clicking of the typewriter calmed me down. I neatly typed out one letter after another and put it in the 'OUT' box to my right. The pile grew steadily, and I hoped I could make up for my absence the previous day.

'Hey, there you are again. Good to see you! Nice, coffee's ready,' called Edgar from the doorway behind me. He poured himself a cup of coffee, humming to himself in the small kitchenette in the corner. With a cup of coffee in his hand and a biscuit in his mouth, he walked to the desk by the window and looked at me, beaming enthusiastically. His jaws grinded and he swallowed the biscuit.

'I see the pile of work is growing smaller already, but then...' Halfway through the sentence, he abruptly stopped speaking. His cup, which he had just brought to his mouth to take the first sip, slumped down again, and his eyes bore into my face. He took a good look at me and asked, 'Say, are you actually better? Shouldn't you be in bed or something? You look lousy.'

Even though I had resolved to pretend nothing was wrong, he must have seen on my face that something terrible was going on. He walked to the door, closed it, and sat down in the chair next to me.

'Tell me, NOW!' he commanded. And I did, surprising myself.

'Show me,' he said next. I did that, too, pulling the scarf down. When he asked if it still hurt, I just nodded.

'Yes, stupid question of mine. I can see that it does.'

Behind me, the door opened, and I heard Freek mutter, G'morning.'

'Can you use my office for a moment?' asked Edgar. 'Kiki and I need to have a chat. All right? Won't take long. I'll come get you in a minute with a fresh cup of coffee, OK?'

'Sure,' Freek said to my back, and the door closed again.

When we were alone again, Edgar poured coffee for me from the large pot in the corner. He put in extra sugar and milk without being asked and set the cup down on the desk in front of me. He placed the opened pack of biscuits next to it.

Holding his own cup between his huge fists, he sat down on the desk chair next to me, brooding. Occasionally, he would glance at me from the side, but he kept quiet until I had drunk some coffee and eaten my first biscuit.

'Just to be sure, don't take it as criticism, but um, the police don't even want to file a police report and they have never wanted to in the past?'

I shook my head no.

'And so, he's never once been properly corrected or punished?'

Again no.

'OK, or actually NOT OK. Don't get mad at me, but would you mind trying to file a report again? I could go with you. Those bruises are, um, impressive. The police can probably do something with that.'

'No,' I said wearily, 'there's no point. I've been there so many times. They'll send me away again, anyway. And my GP's only allowing me to come in when I really have something wrong with me, he said.'

Slowly, we drank our coffee and ate more biscuits. When everything was finished, Edgar said, 'I understand that you can't bring yourself to go to the police again. I'm not much of a fan of them myself, but it can't go on like this. He must understand that he went too far, and that we don't put up with any of this anymore.'

I was grateful to hear that word 'we'.

'Do you mind if I round up some friends to teach him a lesson?'

I looked at him questioningly.

'That we scare him a bit, some threats like you-do-this-then-we-do-that, hurt him a bit maybe.'

'Finish him off,' I replied, 'you have my blessing. But stop, no, of course you shouldn't go to prison for it, so maybe not that.'

'Ah, no, that isn't my intention. Maybe what I propose to do isn't exactly legal. But it won't be lethal and it will hopefully be effective. Only his ego might really be hurt irreparably.' After another long silence, with new cups of coffee on the desk in front of us, he told me more about his plan.

'Look, I wasn't always such a nice guy. I've done things in the past that I'm not so proud of now. For example, before I met my Greetje, I used to snort a line of coke regularly. No, I wasn't addicted, so you don't have to look at me like that. But I was a bit of a wild boy, and I lived without imposing too many limits on myself.

'And with my motorbike friends, we always had a semi-friendly brawl on Friday nights with a motorbike club from Haarlem. Nothing serious, just some bruises and nosebleeds and a few pints of beer before saying goodbye, friends again. The next week, of course, we were back in full force.

'But the police didn't much like what was going on. And we sometimes chased them down together. Just for fun. At least, we thought it was fun at the time. Good rioting against a common enemy. Yes, a few blows were always dealt, even by me. And of course, those officers didn't deserve that; they were just afraid of us. So, I do regret that, although I would still rather walk around the block than run into a cop.

'Those bikes of ours also made an unbelievable noise, and we all looked raw, just scary. Nobody dared to say anything, but in the neighborhood, everybody must have been bothered by us for years and must have been really scared. Afraid of me, too. When I walked down the street, the neighbors would quickly bolt into their gardens and disappear behind their front doors as quickly as possible.

'But since I met Greetje, I look at life differently. She has almost turned me into a decent citizen. And I say that without any regret or rancor. She really has made me a better person. And the vast majority of my friends are now also decent citizens, although they still like to ride their Harleys on the weekends.

'But some of them are still in *the scene*. And because of our bond from the past... well, we are friends for life. And it's those friends I'm going to call for help, if you are OK with that.'

'I guess I am,' I said.

After consulting his diary, Edgar dialed a number. Somebody answered on the other side. '*Kon ta bai?* Yes, man, *mi ta bon*. Listen, can I have a word with you tonight? I have a wonderful job for you. We'll find somewhere suitable in the province. Just having a good chat with someone... *Plaka?*... A hundred guilders, yes, I think we can do that. No problem! ... Uhuh, Friday night is good. A call tonight about the details?'

Questioningly, I looked at him.

'If it goes as planned, I imagine your new boyfriend will meet your father. And this boyfriend will turn out to be a member of a very scary motorclub gang far worse than Hell's Angels. Good?'

Sure, good. After some haggling over who would pay the hundred guilders, we each went to work.

Frank was allowed back in. He looked at me questioningly, but when I didn't say a word, he went to work. Every now and then he would look at me from under his straight hair to check if everything was going well, but he respected the silence and brought me another unasked-for cup of coffee. Amiably, we worked until five o'clock.

A few times during the day, we chatted over the coffee pot. He didn't ask, but it was clear he was trying his best to be extra nice to me. I had left the last two biscuits in the packet for him.

December 1975 – Always in denial

According to him, what other people said was mostly 'not true'. They knew nothing about doing business, making money, or how to invest wisely, let alone how to prepare a tax return correctly. They were, in short, suckers.

In those days, you still filed tax returns on paper forms. And of course, you could get advice on that for a fee, but you could also do it yourself. Of course, he did it himself. He didn't want to give anyone access to his finances and certainly didn't want to pay for advice.

His returns were always creative. 'They should be, because you're robbing yourself if you don't defraud the IRS just a little bit,' he used to say.

Mum, who filed returns with him on the same form, was only allowed to put her signature at the bottom on the dotted line, after he had filled everything in.

When the tax inspector came by to check his records and audit his returns for the past few years, he also thought this official was a sucker, but a potentially dangerous one. Imagine if the man discovered something wrong in his returns.

He forbade the children to speak to the gentleman, and Mum was only allowed to bring him a cup of tea and had to stay in the kitchen. The inspector was not allowed to have a biscuit, because then he would think they were rich and could pay a little more tax.

The sucker did indeed discover some things, though not everything. And although it must have been obvious that he had cheated, he continued to deny that he had. It was a minor omission at most, he insisted. He even got away with it, after paying a modest fine.

When he received the letter from the IRS about the fine, he celebrated this as a great victory. Triumphant, he held it up in the air, and with a red face, shouted to Mum, 'You see, never, NEVER admit you have done anything wrong!' It came out in a long outburst and a cracking voice.

'Really?' Mum said, winking reassuringly at her children, spoiling his good mood.

'OK,' he said, 'marrying you, that was wrong, I'll admit that. Happy now?'

29 August, 1986 – Put on his best behavior

Someone knocked on my door. Strange, it was already evening, and my fellow students had been ignoring me for some time. Cautiously, I crept to the door in my stockinged feet, afraid he would hear me. But through the peep hole in the door, I saw that it was Edgar. I quickly let him in and looked at his outfit in surprise.

He didn't exactly look like his usual self. He normally wore tight-fitting suits, usually with bright silk shirts and neatly polished shoes. Now, he was wearing a long leather jacket and army boots, with big, shiny nails all along the soles. Around his neck was a red handkerchief, and he had obviously not shaved since last Tuesday. He stank of engine, beer, and sweat.

He gave me a huge smile. 'I don't think you'll have any more trouble with that creep for a while.' Then he told his story.

Edgar explained he had called him up and, in his best preppy tone of voice, had introduced himself as my 'boyfriend' wondering whether they could get acquainted sometime soon. He was keen to work on a good rapport with his father-in-law-to-be, as he had understood from

Kiki that family relations were a bit strained. No, Kiki would not come along. Ha-ha, no, bitches only make conversation difficult. Indeed. He was eager for them to get acquainted as men among themselves. Edgar told him that he had to work at the law firm until six o'clock, and afterwards liked to have a bite to eat together in a joint in Elst. Could he come to the car park there on Groenestraat? There, Edgar would pick him up with his company car, and they would go to a restaurant together to eat a nice juicy steak. Edgar (who, incidentally, called himself Willem for the occasion) would of course pick up the tab.

He was too stunned to ask many questions and promised to be there at quarter past six. I think he was also bursting with curiosity and had estimated on the phone that he could handle this nice young lad quite easily. Perhaps he was also interested in the little plan Willem had presented, not too subtly, to bring me to reason once and for all. Or he was just in the mood for a free dinner; it could have been that, too.

A little before six, Edgar and his six biker friends took up their positions in Groenestraat, with a good view of the car park. When he drove up, they started their Harleys and followed him in. They immediately neatly locked his car in with their roaring bikes. He was visibly startled and quickly tried to press the buttons that locked the doors. He succeeded on the driver's side, but Edgar was ahead of him on the passenger side. Calmly, he opened the door.

'Hello, Mr. De Wit. Get out. I'm Willem. We were going to have a chat, weren't we? Let's do so here and now, we're among friends,' he said. 'And if you don't like our chat, you can always decide to skip dinner.'

His friends laughed sardonically, looking forward to what was to come, like a pack of wild dogs smelling easy prey.

When he wouldn't get out himself, Edgar unleashed his friends with a nod. They dragged him out of the car and pushed him against a tree. With big, startled eyes, he looked from one to the other.

'Aaaah, he's afraid of Antilleans,' said the biggest one. 'He just pissed his trousers,' said the scariest. Together they laughed heartily about it. 'Come, come, you are always so brave when you are facing women? Suddenly you can't fight?'

With a dull thud, the first fist landed in his stomach. He immediately dropped to his knees and gasped for breath, his face a picture of disbelief, fear, and bewilderment.

'Yes, that's what it feels like when you get slapped. Sorry, you know, but we're doing this for your own good, ha-ha,' said Edgar, now having dropped his preppy voice. 'You have to experience what it's like for yourself. Somehow, I can't really appreciate you bothering my girl all the time. So, I thought, maybe he just doesn't realize what he's doing. Does he think that with impunity he can make someone weaker than himself do what he wants by force? Is that it? Do you enjoy hurting women, imposing your will on them with your fists? Ah, how pathetic you are now, lying there on your knees in the mud.' He bent down and helped him up.

Edgar then patted his clothes and gave him a friendly look. It looked like they might let him walk away.

His eyes shot from one to the other, trying to figure out if the beating would stop there, and if he could indeed walk away... run away, actually. But he was not that lucky. The friends gathered around him, pushing and shoving him around their circle.

'Yes, take a good look at your daughter's friends,' said Edgar, even less friendly this time. 'If needed, we'd love to come and see you more often. Kiki will tell us when it's time for a visit again, surely you understand?'

Sobbing, he stood in the circle. He had no idea how to make this stop.

After a while, Edgar said to his mates, 'You go ahead and start the Harleys. I'll talk to him a little longer.'

When the friends turned around to go, he was too scared to run. Edgar stepped right in front of him. Now he really didn't look friendly anymore; bloodthirsty more like.

'Listen carefully, you asshole. If you put your dirty paws on Kiki again, you're dead. Understood?'

A cautious nod was his reply.

'UNDERSTOOD, ASSHOLE?'

'Yes,' he said softly, defeated.

Somewhere in the distance, the siren of an approaching police car could now be heard. They had apparently been alerted by local residents. Edgar noisily cleared his throat and spat on the ground, turned around and climbed on the back of one of his friends' bikes. Roaring loudly, they rode out of the parking lot.

'Fuck you!' they shouted in farewell, and, 'Keep your hands to yourself in future, otherwise we will come to visit.'

Within an hour they were in Amsterdam where they dropped Edgar off in front of my student flat. He had thanked his friends profusely and wanted to hand them the promised hundred-guilder note. But they wouldn't take it. They didn't want to be paid for such a nice job. They sent heartfelt greetings to Kiki. Happy to see you next time. Wide grins. *Te aworo!*

July 1976 – Xenophobia

Migrant workers had been coming to the Netherlands since the 1960s, initially mainly Italians and Spaniards, but later also from other countries. They had not consciously experienced this because they were busy emigrating to Australia themselves. But when they returned to the Netherlands after four years, they saw for the first time in their lives what they then unabashedly called 'foreigners'.

In Australia, they had never seen them either, because that country had a strict admission policy for all kinds of population groups. It effectively only allowed in white Europeans from the United Kingdom, Germany, and the Netherlands. The Aboriginals had been safely housed, he said, in areas outside what he called 'the civilized world'; the world inhabited by the white invaders, that is.

But Mum really liked 'other' people. She was curious about their customs and especially their recipes, because she loved cooking. And she wasn't afraid of foreigners either. He was. The fact that foreigners lived everywhere outside the Netherlands, was no problem for him. They were safely tucked away there, as far as he was concerned.

But when his children (actually foreigners in the Netherlands, too, but he never thought of that) were in primary school, it became increasingly common for healthy Dutch families to go abroad for one or two weeks in the summer. Most went to a sunny country, such as France. For the really daring, there were the Spanish *Costas* that were just cautiously beginning to flourish after *El Generalísimo* had started interfering with tourism there. And then, of course, there was Italy. It was further away, the foreigners there – like in Spain – spoke an unintelligible language, but above all it was more expensive. Italy was only for rich people, or so it seemed.

Much to his chagrin, the downstairs neighbors turned out to be a bit more affluent than he had estimated, or at least more affluent than himself. And these downstairs neighbors told him that in the summer they would leave for two months with their sons (the same age as his children) to stay in a villa owned by Dad-in-law near Siena. The garden there was big enough for a tent, and they wondered whether he might fancy coming over with his family for a week or so, too. Oh well, compulsory school attendance wouldn't be so strict for the children. And there was a small pool there as well.

It really sounded too good to be true, especially when it became clear that nothing had to be paid for their stay, since the neighbors didn't pay anything to their in-laws. And together they could take turns looking after the children as well. This, of course, opened up unprecedented prospects!

The old Alpenkreuzer tent trailer was taken out of Grandpa and Grandma's shed and inspected for any insurmountable damages. Of course, this time any leaks, which could not have been missed on previous trips, did not count. After all, it never rains in Italy.

After his approval, the old trailer was dragged home and packed with Dutch food, clean clothes, and bedding. Mum did not feel like going at first, but she was actually excited by the children's holiday mood. She was looking forward to the Italian food, having read many articles about it in *Margriet* and devouring the recipes with her eyes.

In good spirits, the family left for Italy at dusk ('because then the children can sleep'). After only half an hour, the children were wide awake; first the boy and then the girl. Seatbelts didn't exist in the back seats then, so they could stand behind the front seats and ask if they were there yet. And they did. Often.

'Can those children finally SHUT UP NOW!!!!' he shouted angrily every now and then in Mum's ear, who nicely ignored him. Finally, he reached behind his chair and took turns viciously pinching the children's calves.

After a long, hot journey, they arrived in Italy. It smelled exciting and different. They couldn't see much, though, because it was now pitch black again.

They had long since run out of cheese sandwiches, currant buns, and lukewarm apple juice, so they were very hungry and terribly thirsty. Cautiously, the boy inquired if there was another sandwich or a sip of juice left. He got no answer. Mum turned to him and gave him a warning look. The girl didn't dare say she was thirsty.

After another hour of driving, they suddenly saw a brightly lit area with lots of activity, somewhere beside the road. When he had brought the combination of the fully loaded car and tent trailer to a creaking halt, dance music could be heard in the distance.

'I'm going to have a look,' he said to no one in particular. 'You stay here and keep an eye on the trailer.'

Curious, within seconds of his departure, the rest of the family were standing next to the car, eagerly watching what was happening in the distance. It sounded exciting, like a promise. They could just sniff fragrant food fumes, and their hunger and thirst were becoming increasingly difficult to ignore.

After a few minutes of waiting, he returned with one big Italian and two small ones, who all looked rather fierce. The big one shouted something in Italian, which they obviously didn't understand, then poked his finger into the little boy's chest and grinned in the girl's direction. He stank.

The little men inspected the car and trailer, then they too came closer. They made big gestures. With one eye on the car and one eye on Mum and the kids, he watched the spectacle, his arms held unnaturally close to his sides. The little girl was scared and shyly ducked behind Mummy's back. Then the big man gestured for them to follow.

'Just do as he says,' he squeaked, his voice skipping.

In the dark they walked meekly towards the music and the food. A large crowd sat at long tables, schmoozing and devouring strange food. Men, women, children, old and young, all crisscrossed and happily mixed together. On a stage, a small ensemble with accordions was playing dance music.

For a moment, it became dead silent and everybody seemed to look at them from head to toe at the same time. Then, as if agreed, the people at the tables turned back to their plates and continued eating and talking.

They then made room for the Dutch guests; the table was scrubbed with a splash of wine, and large glasses of wine and lemonade and deep plates of pasta were placed on it. The family was gently forced onto benches and expected to attack.

The girl's fear was soon overcome, and she sipped the delicious lemonade. Then she awkwardly started cramming the long, divine strands of red goo into her mouth as quickly as she could with a fork. She had never tasted anything so delicious before, and apparently her brother thought so, too.

The big Italian from earlier bent over the table between the children with a grater and a piece of cheese. It suddenly rained cheese on the pasta. Even more delicious!

Accidentally, a small burp escaped the girl. Mum looked at her warily, but it was no problem. The girl was kindly patted on the head by an elderly lady, who scooped a little more pasta onto her plate and smilingly gestured that she could eat quite a bit more. She also filled the girl's lemonade glass to the brim once more and slid it closer across the table in encouragement, smiling sweetly at the girl with a crooked mouth in which several teeth seemed to be missing.

Her parents sat there somewhat uncomfortably, sipping wine. Politely, they also took a few bites of the pasta Bolognese – an unknown and exotic dish for the average Dutch person at the time.

But after the first bites and sips, they also seemed to appreciate the Italian food. He gobbled it all down and then wiped his plate clean with a piece of baguette, which he swallowed in one go with a few firm gulps of wine. Mum ate in her own fussy way; she chopped the strings of spaghetti into bite-sized chunks, and with the fork she neatly deposited them in her mouth bit by bit and without spilling. But it showed that she was enjoying it more and more. The wine did not miss its mark on her either.

For the children, there were large scoops of lemon ice cream at the end. For the parents, there was *grappa*. But Mum enjoyed some ice cream with her children and passed her glass of *grappa* to him.

Slowly, the children became aware that a large group of women were gathering around them, approvingly appraising the spectacle with their hands crossed over their chests. They came closer and closer. One even briefly touched the boy's blond hair and mumbled something. And the girl's blonde tresses were also felt.

'Now we'll have it,' hissed Mum, suddenly seeming completely sober. And yes, now they were all coming closer. In no time, they were enclosed, and the children were cheered: '*Bambini, bambini!*'

Mum was 'kidnapped' towards the dance floor and had to dance with all the men from the village, and later with the groups of women. At first, she still looked anxiously towards her children, but when she realized that nothing terrible would happen to them among all those smiling Italian *nonnas*, she surrendered to the entertainment.

Meanwhile, he became the center of a heated but incomprehensible debate between the Italian men, and he had to clink with them all in turn and finish his glass. After an hour, he was grinning like a horse and all the men were his *amici*.

It was getting later and merrier all the time. Everyone was laughing, dancing, and singing like crazy. The girl and boy played hide-and-seek with the other children, and were occasionally patted on the cheek by passing women who handed them biscuits, bottles of lemonade, and strange treats in sticky candy wrappers.

Nodding and satisfied, they sat exhausted, waiting for what was to come next. At dawn (had they slept a little?), the girl woke up in the arms of a sturdy granny, who carried her towards the car, where the whole family was seen off by a large crowd. Just before they drove off, they were handed a large packet of delicious sandwiches and a wine bottle full of lemonade, through the open window, for the road.

'Gosh, what incredibly nice people, those Italians,' he said cheerfully, trying to keep the car on course after all the booze. 'And they didn't even want to be paid for the food!' After fifteen minutes of driving, he stopped the car and puked on the roadside.

Arriving at the neighbor's holiday address, he proudly recounted the adventure as if he had arranged it all himself.

'Where was this, exactly?' the neighbor asked.

Hearing the name of the village, he burst out laughing. Hiccupping uncontrollably, he was just able to say that this must have been communist party's annual gathering. 'So, have you joined yet?' he asked.

'No. Of course, I didn't trust those foreigners one bit.'

1 September, 1986 – Student grant

Today was the official start of the new academic year. One of the biggest changes was that all students were now eligible for a government grant of 605 guilders, which was independent of their parents' income. And it was a gift; it didn't have to be paid back later.

I couldn't believe my luck. Together with the money I earned from my job, I suddenly had unprecedented financial freedom and independence. I went home less and less often; in fact, hardly ever. My mother was overjoyed and understood immediately. He understood, too, but of course he didn't accept my not coming home without a fight.

He was angry and almost immediately stopped paying my room rent. That was fine with me. After all, I now had my own income, and I didn't need his money. Every week I received money from the temp agency into my checking account, and once a month the money from the student grant was added to that. The rent subsidy was still paid into his account by the city of Amsterdam, and without his signature I couldn't change that, but I let it be. In my eyes, I soon had a fortune.

After a few weeks, he noticed that stopping his payments for the rent was not having its desired effect. I still didn't obediently come home on weekends as he had expected; of course, he knew nothing about my job. He decided to move on to other measures.

His letter of a week earlier had apparently given him an idea. For several weeks now, I had received letters from him almost daily, telling me delicately that I was and always had been ungrateful. Oh yes, and that I made my mother sad that I came home so little. That he thought it was a shame that I preferred being in Amsterdam to being at home, even though I didn't have lectures on weekends. Did I have the wrong friends, maybe? I had never been virtuous, and if I continued like this, it would end badly for me. And so on, and so forth.

Some of those letters found their way through the mail, but others were in my mailbox without a stamp, or I found them slipped under my door. One of the letters he had even handed to Fenna, who came to give it me in the kitchen with feigned kindness one day when I was cooking. She would have preferred reading what it said over my shoulder, but I folded it into my pocket without saying anything, so she slunk off.

After the fifth letter, I put the envelopes unopened into the bottom of my desk drawer and tried to ignore them. When the pile got too big, I shredded them and flushed them down the toilet one by one.

Then he began lurking around the student flat regularly. But I usually managed to avoid him by checking each time I got home if his car was parked nearby, before sneaking up the fire escape to my room. Once I was safely behind my door, I let him stay in the corridor. The shouting and knocking on the door usually stopped quickly, especially if one of my flat mates showed up.

I thought it best to avoid the communal kitchen. If he found me there, it would be difficult to get rid of him. So, two days a week from then on, I ate in the canteen on Weesperstraat, and on two other days in the new canteen on Binnengasthuisterrein, with students who had no kitchen of their own, or who just didn't feel like cooking.

It was all quite cozy. I soon became a member of the Spotty Nibblers, a group of students who always ate together at weekends.

August 1976 – Weekend terror

'Grandpa and Grandma' were those on his side of the family. Grandpa and Grandma on Mum's side were hushed up for some unfathomable reason. And once they were actually dead, they were never even mentioned again in front of him. In short, there was only one grandma and only one grandpa, and that is where they went every weekend. They often stayed the night there, too, on his orders and with the whole family. So, every Friday evening they set off on a long car journey to the Veluwe, a rural area about sixty kilometers to the east. And if they stayed the night, they would return home in the dark on Sunday evening.

To some extent, the children were fine with that. There was a big garden there for them to romp in, Grandpa had made two swings, and across the street lived two boys of the same age that they could play with. Together they played wild games, just out of sight of grown-ups. The girl tried her best to be as tough as possible, so that she would not be excluded by the boys. But she didn't need to worry. Her brother was always quick to defend her and always let her play along.

From the start, however, the sleepovers posed a big problem.

Grandma always got up before dawn to do the laundry – by hand that is, and on the steps just under the bedroom windows. With her sloshing and thumping, she would wake everyone up. And don't think that, as a child, you can get a wink of sleep then. Certainly not if you are lying in a double bed together with a sibling. The children giggled under the covers, but somehow that always ended in a spanking, because he thought they should be quiet until he too wanted to get out of bed. But he never mentioned the noise under the bedroom window to Grandma, who was the one constantly waking them up after all. It was a good start to a fine day.

Around eleven o'clock, the first nephews and nieces, aunts and uncles arrived. At noon, the family was always complete, and the children were given sandwiches in their hands and told to go into the garden (rain or shine). The women sat in the front room, and Grandpa and Grandma's five sons and Grandpa himself, of course, in the back room. God knows what they talked about, but the result was invariably that around three o'clock in the afternoon the mood was so languid that sherry had to be brought out in the front room and beer in the back room. And there was always a bit of arguing and resentment between the front and back rooms before it got dark. Woe betide any child who had to pee before then and came into sight of one of the uncles or aunts...

By about six o'clock they would all eat together from a big tray of sandwiches that Grandmother, Mum, and the aunts – their cheeks red from the sherry – had prepared in the kitchen. Fortunately, after dinner, most said goodbye and a relative calm returned.

When the girl was about twelve, she no longer felt like being dragged to Grandpa and Grandma every weekend. She was perfectly happy to stay at home for the weekend and told him so him during dinner, safely from across the dining room table. He looked at her dumbfounded.

'What would Grandma think of that?' he asked.

'Nothing, so what?' Her heart was beating in her throat.

'She'll think you don't love her anymore. And you always like coming along, don't you?'

'What makes you think that? I would rather stay at home.'

'Your mother will be lonely if you don't come with us,' he said and fixed his piercing eyes on Mum.

She dropped her eyes from his gaze and said timidly, 'Then I'll stay home, too.'

It hit him like a bomb. As if they had collectively planted a knife in his back, he looked at everyone reproachfully.

And he didn't give up so quickly. Unexpected prodding and every other means of pressure were used by him to force the girl to come along. Pocket money, which incidentally she and her brother received very rarely, was withheld for weeks. Mum was told in every subtle but unmistakable way that she was failing in her obligations as a good mother and daughter-in-law. Or there was no talk at all until it was Friday night. Then he would suddenly cheerfully say, 'Hop into the car, you lot, we're going to Grandpa and Grandma's.' Often, they were all so happy that he was speaking again that they meekly stepped into the car.

Only later, when she entered puberty, did the girl hold her ground, and she sometimes stayed at home despite his tactics. Her brother was often with friends and thus managed to evade the quarrels and the threatening sleepovers. But by then she was happy to spend a week arguing, just to be relieved of his presence all day on weekends.

The only downside was that Mum kept going with him, and she always returned on Sunday evenings looking pale and dejected. Then the girl did feel guilty, even though Mum often told her that she was quite right not to want to go along.

She would have preferred to be on the other side of the world just to avoid experiencing Mum coming home after such a weekend.

25 September, 1986 – Divorce

He loved to own things, but unfortunately hated working. When, like his older brother, he was taken from the vocational school at the age of fifteen by my grandmother and had to work in the local margarine factory, he felt this as a big, personal defeat. Every day he had to be shouted out of bed by Grandma, otherwise he would never have arrived at work on time. Early on, the idea must have occurred to him that he had to get rich as soon as possible and at all costs, and then retire. He could talk about it for hours, ad nauseam, but I was careful not to let on that I was tired of the story.

When my parents got married, they had decided to go with the flow of emigrants to Australia. Money could be made quickly there, and they had succeeded in doing just that. But after almost four years of slogging, they had decided (or was it him again?) to return to the Netherlands with their accumulated savings and my brother and me. There they bought and furnished a flat, and he started working as a curtain rail sales representative, while my mother stayed at home to take care of us children. In Australia she could have worked herself to death for all he cared, but here in the Netherlands it would have been frowned upon for her to have a job outside the home. And besides, there was no need, because he had already laid the foundation for their wealth.

In the end, they owned (excuse me, *he* owned) six houses – spread across the Netherlands and various holiday hotspots in Europe – along with a considerable amount of savings and various investments. This had all been scraped together by depriving not only himself, but also his family, of everything. Ideally, he would have preferred to become the owner and managing director of the curtain rail company that he represented. But that plan did not pan out.

After years of bickering with him over it, my mother started working night shifts in a nursing home for demented elderly people and had a reasonable income. As a result, he decided at the age of forty-five that the joyful day had come when he could stop working. The rental income from 'his' holiday homes, the return on 'his' investments, the interest on 'his' savings, and my mother's salary (also 'his'), added together were enough to live on. And early retirement as a pensioner sounded even better than managing director!

Their marriage imploded when their sudden, daily closeness threatened to become even more oppressive, as he suddenly appeared to have rented out their house to strangers without consulting Mum and they would have to live in his smallest holiday home. When packing the moving cartons, my mother set aside three boxes of her personal belongings. On the day before Ascension – just before the moving van was due to arrive – she fled the house with those three boxes. She bivouacked for a few months with my brother Bram, who kept the door firmly locked, did not respond to the ringing phone, and tore up his letters unread.

After a few months, the separation was final and they were officially divorced. If he had expected my mother to come back to him, it was a miscalculation. She stood firm and moved into a small flat in Leusden, close to her work.

Out of pure envy, he demanded all assets at the divorce; after all, she had never worked as hard for them as he had. And he was successful in his efforts, because he had never reported a large part of those assets to the tax authorities, so my mother could not prove that there were bank accounts and holiday homes abroad.

September 1976 – Taking over the business

He did not particularly like colleagues; he preferred to work alone. As a sales representative selling curtain rails, he could do whatever he wanted without being watched. 'I am my own man,' he used to say. But in the long run it was also a bit boring. No one was judging him, except for maybe a disgruntled customer whom he just simply dumped. But vice versa, he couldn't nag anyone during work either. So he made up for that at home in the evening.

Then one day something exciting happened. The company he represented selling curtain rails was taken over by a much larger company. Suddenly, items like DIY tools, plastic ponds, and garden chairs joined the range.

The new owner offered him permanent employment, but in return he expected Mr. De Wit to simply sell the entire range, but in a smaller catchment area. This, of course, immediately pissed him off. Just imagine: others would take over most of his customers, and he would have to sell items that he was not interested in to new customers. And they hadn't even mentioned the fact that a smaller catchment area would inevitably lead to less travel, and consequently less travel expenses he could claim (and, of course, his gross overestimation of travel expenses would be more noticeable).

At home, he had never really been fun to be with. But now things got really bad until there was a rumor that the curtain rail division was going to be sold.

He went to great lengths trying to buy the division and start his own company, preferably with one or two salespeople. His plan was to fire them in due course, when his son was old enough to join him in the company. Mum could do the accounts, and his daughter could help prepare all sales orders for shipping. He had it all figured out in his mind. What exactly he – the managing director! – would do, except supervise (in other words, get in everyone's hair), remained unclear.

His son listened disdainfully and pointed out that the division was not being sold for nothing. After all, it was not doing well. Everyone wanted modern blinds – horizontal or vertical, it didn't matter. And so there was much less demand for curtain rails. But far more importantly, the boy had no desire to work for his father, thank you very much. By now, the boy was so big and strong that he didn't dare to touch him. Mum got his share.

The girl kept her mouth shut but vowed not to lift a finger to send his damned packages anywhere. She had just entered grammar school and worked hard to get her diploma so she could go to university. If at all possible, in rooms. Away from home.

Mum was not at all keen on the adventure either and said that if he wanted to take over that shitty company, then by all means he could – but on his own. He should just hire people, but not think that the rest of the family would work for him. Slavery had been abolished some time ago!

After many a bitter quarrel, it turned out that a financially exorbitant bid had been made for the curtain rail division by a Belgian investor. And they didn't want to employ him. Instead of a directorship in his own company, he got the consolation prize. He continued to do the same work for his current employer, but was now allowed to use a new job title: *sales manager*. And now he no longer had to sell curtain rails.

To the outside world, he managed to present this as a great victory and an excellent promotion. Proudly, asked and unasked, he showed the pre-printed business cards with his new job title. But behind closed doors, it was Mum's and the kids' fault that an excellent opportunity had been taken away from him. And when the curtain rail company went bankrupt two years later, he claimed that would never have happened if he had taken over. He thought it was a crying shame that his life's work had been ruined in this way with mismanagement by the new owner.

And that, too, was his family's fault, of course.

20 April, 1987 – Easter Bunny

It was Easter Monday, and I was sitting on Edgar and Greetje's sofa with a big mug of hot cocoa. 'I really don't want to appear nosy, mind you, but don't you actually go visit your parents on holidays?' asked Greetje.

'Well, no, my parents divorced last year. It's just very difficult, and it wasn't that easy before the divorce either. '

'What a pity. You only have one set of parents. A good family bond is very valuable, and surely this divorce shouldn't make any difference to how you treat them? My parents are dead, and I would give an arm and a leg if I could get them back. I miss them terribly, even though we had arguments sometimes, too.'

Carefully, I put my mug on the table in front of the sofa. 'Um, thanks very much for the fun, but now I have to go,' I said and stood up.

Edgar had just walked in with a plate of stuffed eggs and looked from one to the other of us in surprise. 'You're not going to leave just when things are getting cozy, are you?'

'Sorry, I really have to leave now,' I whispered, and walked around him. I grabbed my coat off the rack and stormed out the door.

Behind my back I heard Greetje hissing something to Edgar. 'Jesus!' yelled Edgar, just as I stepped off the garden path.

I was already at the end of the street when Edgar caught up with me. 'Stop, please, stop!' he said. 'She doesn't know. She meant well. She really would never have said anything if she had known. Don't leave,' he begged.

He saw my tears and pressed a large white men's handkerchief into my hand. 'Tut, tut, come back with me, please.' He put his arm around my shoulders and with gentle coercion turned me around and took me back to his house.

Greetje was shocked when she heard the story. Edgar told it; I didn't have to say anything. It was just as well, because I couldn't have. There was dead silence for a while after he had finished, then Greetje said, 'Sorry, sorry, sorry.' And she gave me a firm hug.

'No, I am the one to say sorry. You can't help it that I asked Edgar to keep you out of it.'

'Well, that's a secret he's kept well hidden from me. But in this case, I'll forgive him.'

Edgar looked almost relieved. He held the plate of stuffed eggs under my nose. 'Here, take one, stop crying. You'll always be welcome here, do you hear?'

I put an egg in my mouth, and soon another. With some wine to go with it, I began thawing a little.

'And do you know what the Easter Bunny brought?' He handed me a small, shiny piece of paper with a faint, square black-and-white picture on it. 'Isn't it simply great? No, you are holding it upside down; you'll see better if you turn it,' he said, and both he and Greetje looked at me expectantly.

I looked closely at the picture again but could not immediately detect anything in it. It looked like a Rorschach stain. And surely now I had to say what I saw in it, or something like that.

Suddenly I saw that above the stain there was a name, printed in small letters (M.J. de Jong) and two dates, apparently a date of birth and yesterday's date. At the top right was also the abbreviation OLVG. I got it. It was a picture they had made during a pregnancy ultrasound at Onze Lieve Vrouwen Gasthuis Hospital. Of Greetje, of course, whose full name was Margaretha Johanna de Jong.

'Jesus, Edgar! Greetje! Congratulations!' We danced around the room together as we took turns looking at the picture and at Greetje's belly. They were looking forward to the baby, who was due on 20 December, and who they vowed they would take good care of.

October 1976 – The guardian

The children had to be well taken care of, he thought. So, one day he decided that something needed to be arranged in case he was suddenly no longer around. Mum said nothing.

In his will, he wanted to appoint a guardian. He wanted one of his four brothers to take on this task. Luckily, he chose a nice uncle.

After a long car ride, during which, as usual, he did not speak at all, they arrived in distant Friesland. There, the matter would be discussed with the uncle, at his home. Soon after arriving, the girl and boy were sent out of the room, and after much throat-clearing, which was clearly audible in the corridor, he got to the point. The uncle's murmur was just a little harder to understand than his hoarse voice, but it didn't sound angry or surprised, so brother and sister exchanged pleased looks in the hallway. They took turns peeking through the small window next to the door to see what was happening. They saw that, with a grand gesture, he took an envelope from his inside pocket and gave it to their uncle, who had a puzzled look on his face and placed it on the dining room table.

'What would be in there?' the girl whispered to her brother.

He looked happy. 'A lot of money, of course,' he said. 'And then we can live here forever.'

'So, could Mummy stay here, too?' the girl asked.

Hand-in-hand, the children waited for what would happen next.

But alas, after dinner they were packed into the car and, again shrouded in deep silence, he drove home. The children had imagined something quite different. Crying, they had said goodbye to their uncle and reluctantly walked to the car. From behind the car windows, they saw their uncle watching them leave with a strange look on his face.

Years later, the uncle told the then already grown-up children that he had opened the envelope immediately after the car drove down his garden path. He was bursting with curiosity after seeing the theatrical text: 'To be opened after my death'. Inside was a note that began: 'If you're reading this, I won't be here anymore,' with a description of how something valuable could be found in the crawl space under the third tile from the hatch in the garage. The uncle had shown the note to his three other brothers, and they had laughed heartily about it together.

The uncle never knew what was under the third tile on the right in the crawl space, but Mum and the children did. When he started accumulating money, he felt it should be invested wisely, i.e., in things the tax authorities did not know about. So he opted for bearer bonds. They turned out to fit well in preserving jars, which could then be stored beautifully, tucked in the crawl space under the house.

He had earmarked one of those jars for the uncle. But only if he himself died and the uncle took custody of the children, of course.

Incidentally, the bearer bonds turned out not to be resistant to the condensation that collected underground in the preserving jars. After a few years, some of the bonds had perished. He found this out one day when, like a true Uncle Scrooge McDuck, he wanted to make an inventory of his possessions. A woeful curse rose from the crawl space, and for days he looked as if he had choked on an orange that his gut could not pass. The half-decayed bonds lay drying on the radiators all over the house, spreading a pungent, moldy smell.

He was embarrassed at the thought of having to take the smelly documents to the bank to get money in return. Then, of course, he would have to confess that he had buried them in the crawl space. He worked Mum until she took them to the bank.

26 August, 1987 – Sticking my nose in

On Wednesday afternoons, the city center was busy. Mothers came shopping with their offspring, and they all used the tram. It seemed as if they were all just in that one tram from Overtoom. I had boarded there after some typing at the Municipal Insurance Department.

Usually I had no problems with some noise, but today I found the children's screaming terrible. And the noise produced by the mothers was no less irksome. I tried with all my might to shut myself off from it, but that didn't work very well.

Halfway through the ride, two of the mothers got into an argument about something. They started shouting loudly. 'Keep your kids in check, you stupid bitch,' shouted one. 'Shut up, you cunt,' sneered the other, 'or I'll hammer your mouth shut for you.' And she immediately set out to do just that.

Just then, we arrived at Leidseplein, and I quickly got out, happy to escape.

When the doors closed again, the tram moved on and I was face to face with Fenna, who was sitting just at the front on one of the terraces on Leidseplein. She blushed furiously and tried to look away. But just then, he walked up, kissed her long on the mouth, and sat down in the chair opposite her. Like an adolescent in love, he kept looking at her as she squirmed uncomfortably on her chair and tried to avoid my glances. He didn't see me.

With a jerk, I turned and walked down Leidsestraat, away from the spectacle.

'What were you doing on Leidseplein?' he asked me around six o'clock, when I was cooking in the communal kitchen and he had suddenly walked in. 'You have no business there, you should be studying.'

'I should be asking what you were doing there, and with whom,' I said, continuing to stare into the pan I had on the cooker.

I should have kept my mouth shut. He reached to hit me hard on the side of my head. Out of the corner of my eye, I saw his fist coming at me, and I tried to turn my head away. Too late. He hit my nose full on and immediately stormed out of the kitchen, almost running over Fenna in the process.

With big, startled eyes, she looked at me. She tore off a sheet of kitchen paper, folded it in half, and offered it to me. 'You, um, have a bloody nose. Take this.'

I didn't go to my GP. She did; for a morning-after pill. Soon she had found another room, and I only saw her three more times after that.

November 1976 – Lassie bites

One day, when they were staying with Grandpa and Grandma, the boys across the street called the children over to come and play in their garden. Once there, they saw Lassie was visiting, or at least a dog that looked just like Lassie from the television. This one, though, was a male dog, but the girl did not see that.

'You can pet him,' said the oldest boy next door, 'he won't do anything.'

However, Lassie didn't think that was a good plan. Even before her hand touched his soft fur, the beast spun its head and bit her on the head. It happened so fast, she only saw its huge teeth in a flash. She barely felt anything. Startled, the beast then darted away through the hedge.

'Oh no!' said her brother.

'Yikes, I am going to puke,' said the oldest neighbor boy, while the youngest just looked straight over her head, trying not to see anything.

To stop the bleeding, which by now was gushing from several holes in the girl's head, her brother took off his t-shirt, and pressed it hard on his sister's head. It worked. In the end there wasn't much blood, but the t-shirt had become quite dirty.

After giving the matter some thought, they rinsed it out in the pond in the neighbors' back garden, then let it dry on the stove in the shed. While the t-shirt lay drying, the boy just put on his jumper over his bare chest, and they played the wildest version of tag they could think of.

When Grandma started shouting that dinner was ready, the children crossed the street with innocent looks on their faces, but she wasn't fooled. She immediately noticed that the girl was quite battered and that her grandson's t-shirt was quite dirty.

Within seconds she had gotten what had happened out of them. She first slapped both children around their ears, and then made them eat their dinners in silence. Immediately after they'd eaten, they were sent to bed for punishment. She didn't clean the wounds on the girls' head; a cold flannel on them to prevent the worst swelling was enough.

'No one was ever sick during the war,' she always said. To her, illness was posturing. And hygiene had to be basic and was certainly not focused on the human body, but more on a shiny kitchen sink, white sheets and shirts, and a scrubbed doorstep.

In short, the holes started to become inflamed within a day. Mum dabbed at them with disinfectant for days, until no more pus came out and the infection was over.

He was terribly angry and forbade his children ever to set foot across Granny's street again. They had no business there, according to him. And not even once did he deign to look at the plaster cast on his son's arm.

31 August, 1987 – Manipulation by suicide

It was a cold Monday evening, and I was sitting in the kitchen chilling a bit until my pan of soup had warmed up. Carefully, I felt my nose again. It looked like it was slightly crooked, and it hurt quite a bit. Shit. Now I would have a weird nose for the rest of my life.

Suddenly the caretaker stood in front of me. 'Um, sorry, but are you Kiki de Wit?' he asked.

'Yes, why? Have I done something that is not allowed? My bike is neatly in the rack, isn't it?'

'No, my dear girl, it is not that. Please sit down. I don't have very good news for you.'

I plopped limply on a kitchen chair. 'No, is something wrong with Bram? What happened?' I cried, panicking.

'Is your father's name Bram? I just got a call from the hospital in Apeldoorn. Your father has been admitted there, and he doesn't seem to be doing very well. He asked for you.'

Big relief. So, Bram was OK. Confusing. So now I was expected to go to Apeldoorn all of a sudden. Where was this hospital? And what had happened? Was he maybe dying! Gosh. Was I supposed to cry or laugh now?

The caretaker shoved a piece of paper under my nose with the address of the hospital and the ward where I could find him. Then he walked out of the kitchen without saying anything else. Apparently, he thought his job was done. I crumpled the note in my clenched fist.

I sat at the kitchen table wondering what to do. One by one, other students came into the kitchen to prepare their meals. I ignored them and they me.

When my soup started boiling over, I turned off the heat under the pan, grabbed a spoon from the drawer, and took everything to my room. There I carefully spooned the red-hot soup into my mouth, right out of the pan, and thought about what my options were.

First, I called Bram. Alas, no answer. The only other option was to call Edgar. Fortunately, he answered immediately. I told him about the caretaker and his note.

Half an hour later, he was at my door. 'Do you want to go there?' he asked.

'No, not really. Should I?'

'You don't have to, of course. But maybe it will be the last time you see him, right? You should not go for him, but for yourself. I'd go myself, I think.'

I hesitated.

'My car is in front. I can take you. Greetje knows I will be late.'

Against my better judgement, I let myself be persuaded and we drove along a deserted motorway to Apeldoorn. The closer we got, the less appetite I had for this adventure, but we found the hospital straight away. From the motorway, all we had to do was follow the blue signs with the white H, which was easy, and there was suddenly no time for doubt.

At the night desk, we asked where Mr. De Wit lay. A stern nurse with thick, black-rimmed glasses on the tip of her nose gave me a piercing look.

'Are you family?' she asked.

'Yes, I am his daughter.'

She didn't ask who Edgar was. After another piercing look, she referred us to ward 3A.

At the door to the ward, we met my brother. His face was like thunder. But when he saw me, he was able to smile again.

'Hey, Kiek. I already tried calling you, but you didn't answer. And actually, you could have stayed at home. It's really just a bad theater show here.' He rolled his eyes.

It was a little strange. He and Edgar shook hands. 'This is my friend Edgar, from Amsterdam. He drove me here. What's going on, do you know?'

'Well, actually there's not that much going on. That awful man in there has scratched his wrists a bit with a potato peeler. None too deep, really. Then he quickly called an ambulance himself. And now he's lying here feeling very sorry for himself. It didn't even take stitches to close those scratches, just bandages. Really! Those paramedics must have seen that; they could have just left him at home.

'The first thing he asked when I came in was if you and Mum were coming, too. At his request, one of the nurses had called you, me, and Mum. He had a card with his FAMILY's phone numbers for emergencies in his wallet. Yes, and only I turned up.'

Fleetingly, I wondered why he'd had my Mum called. Surely they were divorced for a very good reason, so what else did he want from her? Fortunately, she was working the night shift and was asleep during the day. She probably wouldn't have heard the phone, thank goodness.

'He has been crying barrels full of tears. We don't understand him, and he has been so lonely since the divorce. Furthermore, you allegedly sabotaged a new relationship, and then he no longer saw a way out. Pathetic, but it's our fault, boo-hoo, and so on. Do you understand that bit about a new relationship?'

In a few words, I recounted what I had seen on Leidseplein, and what had happened later in my kitchen. I pointed to my still slightly swollen nose.

'This Fenna is one of the students in your flat, isn't she?' asked Bram. 'How very distasteful.'

'Yes. Yesterday she left her room with all her stuff. Nobody knows where she is.'

'And so now that his girlfriend has abandoned him, he wants to manipulate us to feel sorry for him with this so-called suicide attempt? Come on, we're leaving. Let the bastard rot!'

I thought this was a great idea, as I didn't feel like entering ward 3A at all. And I did not.

Together with Edgar, we left the hospital. At the entrance, we said goodbye. Edgar gave my arm an encouraging squeeze and then drove back to Greetje, and I went with Bram to Utrecht. On the way, he asked if Edgar was just a friend or my boyfriend. He hoped the latter.

I explained who Edgar was and what he and his friends had done for me the previous summer. After I had told the story, Bram whistled appreciatively. 'That's really nice!' He was sorry that Edgar wasn't my boyfriend, but glad that he was my friend, nonetheless. And we both laughed at the threats made by the so-called biker gang and how they had gotten him to meet them.

The next day, his farewell letter with the treasure map was delivered to both Bram and me. I ignored what it said, but I was especially disgusted by the ending ('Your loving father').

Later, I heard that he had been discharged from the hospital that very day as they couldn't do anything for him medically. And because he demanded extraordinary amounts of time and attention from everyone yet refused a meeting with a psychologist (according to him, they were all half-wits trying to understand themselves a little better), he had to leave. The hospital was not some kind of holiday home.

December 1976 – Even more holiday homes

The history of the holiday home repeated itself. He came in during dinner and said, 'Hello there! Good news. I bought two houses in Spain today.'

'God help us,' Mum said.

'Geez,' said the boy.

The girl said nothing, but made her way out of the room as fast as she could. Safely at the top of the stairs, she listened, with a heart pounding in her throat, to what was happening. But there was little to listen to because nothing else was said. Only the distasteful sound of his slurping and smacking (something he never did in front of other people) filled the silence, which was otherwise brutal.

A week later, when he started talking sparingly again, they heard that this time he had bought not existing, but yet-to-be-built, houses from a Dutch firm that would build all kinds of holiday homes for Dutchmen on a hill near Denia. Of these, he had bought two, straight from the drawing boards. According to him, these would be palaces. And the building firm would also provide a communal swimming pool. This last bit of his story sounded tempting indeed.

But they shouldn't tell anyone at school about anything, '...Because then people would just get jealous.' It was immediately clear to his children that this was, in fact, a gag order.

How could other people know that when the houses were finally finished, they were going to Spain every year from then on to paint, clean, and otherwise make themselves useful, but certainly not to have their holidays there. And that's exactly what people were jealous of: all those holidays!

In those days, it was almost a sport to get as tanned as possible during holidays. Hordes of holidaymakers flocked to the Spanish *Costas* to do virtually nothing but lie on an air mattress in the sun all day and turn over every now and then. The boy disparagingly called the women who did this 'French toast'.

When the girl did not reappear at all sun-kissed at school after the so-called holidays, her classmates attributed this to her blonde hair and pale skin. She just had a tough time tanning. Too bad, you know.

But these so-called holidays only began after a year or so, because the Dutch contractor who had seemed so solid went bankrupt, and a Spanish contractor had to complete the construction. As yet unsold houses were sold to the locals in Spain. And although a communal swimming pool remained in the plans, the entire building plan had to be scaled down, because the Spanish purchases did not yield as much as sales to the Dutch. Instead of wide roads with neat green strips, there would be narrow roads with no plantings. And construction was delayed, with no guarantees given about the completion date.

This, of course, was another source of bitter reproaches back and forth between him and Mum. Somehow, he always managed to explain it in such a way that it was all her fault, and this had to be punished by prolonged and emphatic silence on his part – something he was now extremely adept at. Instead of talking, he would occasionally hand out a vicious poke, when one of the family members did something he obviously didn't like.

Be that as it may, the houses were finished at some point anyway, and from then on the family went to Spain every year to plod along. The children were supposed to be very happy about that, 'because not everyone went to Spain every year anyway.'

'No,' the girl secretly thought, 'they are the lucky ones.' Although she had said nothing, it showed on her face how she felt, and he yanked her up from her chair by her arm until his nose almost touched hers.

'A little gratitude could go a long way, you know,' he said.

She smelled his sour breath and was disgusted. He immediately pushed her off again, causing her to clumsily fall back on the chair. 'Ouch,' she thought, rubbing a hand over her sore arm.

They always drove the almost two thousand kilometers to Denia in one stretch, in a fully packed car. The journey was on hot B-roads where there was no toll to pay but where, according to him, there was a lot to see. They had to take for granted that the journey was a lot slower than on the straight, wide toll motorways. And what was there to see? Well, you don't see that much from a moving car.

By the way, the car was never full of clothes and beach gear and such, but with paint, brushes, cleaning materials, and of course Dutch ('nice and cheap') food.

Every day at breakfast, he handed out the 'chores'. His children only had time to swim in the communal pool at the foot of the *urbanización* in the afternoon, after all their chores had been done and he had inspected and approved the results.

Of course, he presented each outing to the pool as a reward for what he considered to be light chores. They did not get money for an ice cream, though. Late in the afternoon, he would stop by the pool himself and then, with a grand gesture, pull out his wallet to treat them to an ice cream. It would then be up to his son and daughter to put on a happy face so that everyone could see what a great father he was.

Whether they were just splashing in the water or sleeping in the stiff grass, it didn't matter. They were supposed to enthusiastically jump up when he approached with his money and exude the right ice cream craving. Even if they had just been treated to ice cream by a beautiful Juan or José, who were happy to show some adolescent interest in a blonde Dutch chick and who generously also gave her equally blond brother an ice cream. She knew they were really nice boys, just wanting to speak to her with hand gestures and the occasional English or Spanish word; nothing else. They didn't expect anything in return, except a little company. With her brother, they talked in broken English about Johan Cruijff, Ruud Gullit, Barça, or Real Madrid. It was fun, and there were no ulterior motives.

But of course, he told the boys to RUN straight away. Perhaps this was his second reason for always coming down to the pool in the afternoon: to chase away any boys from his kitten like an angry tomcat. He then always looked scornfully at his son. His son should have understood, even without a direct order, that he had to keep those boys away from his sister.

When even he realized after several trips that Spain was quite a long way away, he concluded, after difficult negotiations with Mum, that they had to stay overnight at least once along the way. And on one such trip, they did stay over in a bargain hotel somewhere on the border between France and Spain.

The hotel was called *Hotel Colón*. If Columbus had known what his name was being misused for, surely he would have turned in his grave. But he didn't know what Colón meant, and during the long, hot ride he lectured that it was a hotel where travelers came to stay in columns. What was good enough for others would surely be good enough for them.

The family slept together in one large family room, which contained a double and two single beds. The double bed sagged to the floor. One cot was meant for a toddler, that's how small it was. And the other one looked like a pyre, because of all the pieces of wood screwed and nailed to it to hold the frame together. Sleeping was near impossible on those uncomfortable beds. Moreover, the room stank pungently of urine from the bathroom. And showering was a challenge: only a very small jet of lukewarm water came out of the shower head.

Breakfast consisted of a jug of instant coffee and a few pieces of baguette for the adults, and large plates of porridge with lumps for the children. They were just about to turn up their noses at it when they saw his stare. So, they obediently emptied their plates, just swallowing everything without chewing. They could just about do it without gagging. Mum, meanwhile, nibbled obediently on a piece of baguette. But that one experience at the hotel was enough. Never again!

Some months later, he was cheerfully able to report that he had found the solution to the hotel accommodation problem. Halfway down the journey to Spain, in France's Dordogne region, he had bought two more holiday homes. This time, they were not new ones, but 'existing cottages in the woods'. Hovels, they understood immediately, which of course again needed a lot of work and about which they could tell no one so that no one could become jealous, et cetera.

From then on, they dragged themselves back and forth every holiday between the houses and cottages in Spain, France and, last but not least, the Netherlands.

25 December, 1987 – Christmas presents

Strange, the lights were off and no one answered the door, no matter how many times I pressed the bell. From the window next to the front door, I looked straight into the corridor. Empty. Dark. Could I maybe be a day early? Surely not. It was actually Friday, 25 December, Christmas Day. And I was supposed to arrive at five, wasn't I?

It was bad enough that I hadn't been able to work that day and therefore hadn't been able to earn anything. A Christmas dinner would have been more than welcome. Especially since I had also already spent some money on a few small Christmas presents. Would Greetje have given birth now after all? No, surely I would have heard, wouldn't I?

Undecided, I stood in at the door, trying to decide whether to leave or wait a little longer. Just then, a car turned into the street. Honking happily, it drove towards me. Behind the windshield, a large white palm was waving at me.

In front of the door, Edgar stepped out. Smiling broadly, he walked towards me, hugged me enthusiastically, and pressed two awkward kisses on my cheeks. 'It's great you're here, Kiki. You have the scoop. I'll help them inside first and then you can meet Edgar junior. Born last night at one minute past midnight, almost a week late, but perfectly healthy. And so, he's also a real Christmas child like you! Hold on,' he reached past me and unlocked the front door. 'Go on in. If you turn on the lights and light the Christmas tree, we'll be right in.'

Without waiting further for my reply, he turned to the car and I walked inside. At the back of the corridor was the door to the living room. After some fumbling with nervous fingers, I managed to switch on the ceiling lamp and also the lights on the Christmas tree. Nervously, I stood in the middle of the room.

A few minutes later, Edgar and his wife Greetje walked in. She was leaning heavily on Edgar's arm, but she was glowing with happiness. In his left arm, Edgar was holding a small, white bundle, wrapped in a blanket. It had to be Edgar junior. Once Greetje had been carefully installed on the couch by Edgar, she opened the white package and they looked endearingly together at the baby that emerged. It really was a beautiful baby, I saw with shock.

'I can see that it is not very convenient that I'm visiting now. I'll pull the door shut behind me, though. Many congratulations.'

'Are you joking? You're not leaving,' said Edgar. 'It's not your fault that Greetje gave birth a little later than planned. We are very happy to have you here. You are just like family. And you know better than anyone what it's like to be a Christmas child, don't you?'

'Yes, do stay!' said Greetje, beaming. 'I suddenly went into labor yesterday afternoon and, well, a little after midnight this little guy was born. It all went amazingly fast. I'm a natural, they said at the hospital. And I'm not tired at all, just very hungry.'

'Okay, okay,' Edgar said. He understood the hint. 'I'll see what we have for dinner. It won't be an elaborate Christmas dinner, though, and we don't have rusks with aniseed sprinkles to celebrate the birth, because we haven't been able to do the shopping. Here, I'll take your coat with me right away. Sit down, please.'

Greetje patted the sofa next to her. 'Would you like to hold him for a moment?'

Fascinated, I looked at the child. It was a human being in the making; in miniature, that is. But after a minute, Greetje wanted to hold him again herself.

'There's my little man,' she whispered tenderly. It brought a lump to my throat. Really.

After a few minutes, Edgar walked back into the room. He was wearing a colorful kitchen apron with red ruffles. And he used a large ladle to reinforce all his words. 'I'm going to make a nice omelet. There is also soup, and eating dessert is also possible. Do you eat pork?'

'Yeah, nice, but don't make too much of a fuss.'

'No fuss, we're going to celebrate! My parents are still on Curaçao, Greetje's are dead, and yours are... well, they are not here. But we're going to make something of it together tonight.' After casting another beaming glance at 'his two darlings' on the sofa, he disappeared back into the kitchen.

As I was setting the table, we heard Edgar singing Christmas carols in the kitchen, loudly and out of tune. After a while, there was a lovely smell. From time to time, Edgar looked around the corner of the door to see how we, and especially Junior, were doing. 'Hey, come on, relax a bit now. We're so happy together, and you're celebrating with us, aren't you?'

I decided to enjoy myself as much as I could, and gave in.

The food was delicious. First there was a spicy soup, then a pork patty, followed by an omelet with spinach, and then a slice of ice cream cake – all doused for Edgar and me with plenty of red wine. And for Greetje, who lay comfortably on the couch with the baby on her lap, with large glasses of warm aniseed milk.

'Good for milk production, ha-ha,' she said cheerfully, rubbing her voluminous bosom meaningfully.

While Edgar and I took our last bites of the ice cream cake, she breastfed Junior. Occasionally, appreciative smacking sounds could be heard. Not only from the baby, by the way, because everyone was eating and drinking to their heart's content.

Around eight o'clock, Greetje started nodding off, and Edgar and I were quite tipsy.

'Before I forget, I brought you some Christmas presents,' I said. They loved the baby jumper and the red fire engine. From Edgar, there was a new dressing gown under the tree for Greetje. And she handed him a small parcel with a new watch in it.

'And we have a birthday present for you, of course,' Edgar said. 'Sorry, but we ran out of time to wrap it nicely. Hopefully you can forgive us.'

He handed me a plastic bag from De Bijenkorf department store, and inside was a red jumper. I enthusiastically thanked both Edgar and Greetje, and I wore that jumper until it was worn down to the thread.

January 1978 – Birthday present

He loved money and so could only part with it with great difficulty. Even if it was scorching hot, they would never have a drink on a terrace. 'Just drink from the tap when you go to the toilet later,' he would say. Objections that you just couldn't go to the toilet anywhere, because it was only for paying customers, he simply ignored. Eating ice creams together then? No. At most, a family pack was bought at Jamin's candy shop and then devoured at home (the children and Mum a small bowl each; him the rest).

Gift-giving was also something he thought was a bummer. And tricky, too, because it was difficult to give someone a present for as little money as possible yet which still looked as grand as possible. Gifts for his parents, of course, had to compare most favorably with those of his four brothers. So, for days before Grandpa and Grandma's birthdays, he was already nervous about what he was going to give them.

It was a happy coincidence that the company he had sold curtain rails for presented nice promotional gifts for good customers. As a sales representative, he had always kept a modest stock in hand, and at the time when he quit, he had kept back the best of them. The very best (i.e., the most expensive) gifts were the table lighters with a casing of colored glass. He had unwrapped them one by one at home and lined them up on the dining table to look at and to show them to the girl and boy. Then he took out the prettiest one, wrapped it in a gift wrap, and put it away in his bookcase.

A few weeks later, when they were preparing to leave for Grandpa's birthday that day, he took the parcel out of his bookcase. He stood impatiently at the front door, holding it in his hand, waiting for Mum to get her make-up right. The children were already waiting resignedly by the car with their coats on.

On the way in the car, they had made goofy faces at each other, making sure he couldn't see them in the mirror.

'Nicked it, and now he's going to give that thing to Grandpa,' the boy had whispered in his sister's ear.

'Dad, are you going to give that lighter to Grandpa?' she asked innocently.

'Yes,' he said. 'Beautiful, isn't it? I'm sure Grandpa will be happy with it.'

'But, Daddy, it's a gift for customers, isn't it?' she asked.

'Those customers are long gone,' Dad said. Then he patted Mum's knee and looked at her lovingly from the side.

They arrived last. All the uncles, aunts, and other grandchildren were present and had already handed their presents and drawings to Grandpa. Coolly, they greeted the new arrivals. But then they spotted the bruise on Mum's eyebrow and the mood brightened. You just had to laugh at such clumsiness. What had she bumped into this time? Ha-ha, what a blind chick she was.

Only Uncle Hans didn't laugh; he just looked sternly at his brother who, as usual, totally ignored him. Uncle Hans had no sense of humor, he always told his family. He had never married either, because he fell for men. So why should he interfere with Mum and Dad's marriage? He should just keep his mouth shut and find himself a nice wife, then his antics would be over, he said. And of course, he had no right to spoil any of their fun.

All this took place while everyone was busy consuming lemonade and cake. Tensely, the children looked to see if some cake had been left for them. Of course, it had. Grandma had set aside two big pieces of whipped cream cake for them, and they eagerly sunk their teeth into the sweet goodness. Meanwhile, with a serious face, he shook hands with his brothers (except with Uncle Hans, who seemed to hiss angrily at him), kissed aunties chastely on their cheeks, and positioned himself in the most visible place in the living room, diagonally behind Grandpa's chair.

'Here it comes,' the boy whispered, licking his sticky fingers one by one and then wiping them on his trousers.

And yes, like a rabbit out of a top hat, he conjured up his present from behind his back. With a wide gesture, he handed it to Grandpa, who opened it with a slightly ironic look on his face.

'What a beautiful lighter. Thank you very much. Have another drink.'

'That's what Daddy gives to his customers, too,' the boy said, clearly audible.

The words dropped like a bombshell, and for Dad there was nothing left to say to save face. One of the aunts choked on her sherry and another spontaneously had a fit of laughter, which she immediately tried to stifle by coughing noisily into her handkerchief. After a deep silence, the party went on as if nothing had happened.

He couldn't laugh about it. Neither could his son, after he had 'explained' to him at home in the evening in great detail, and 'for his own good', what he had done wrong.

8 January, 1988 – The motorbike

The day after Bram's final exams, he moved to rooms in Utrecht. Before his flight, he had earned a few hundred guilders washing cars, cutting grass in the gardens on the new housing estate where we lived, and selling the most expensive stamps from his album. Soon, he found a job in Utrecht as a waiter in one of the hip little bars in a dank cellar on Oude Gracht Canal, where cheap wine was poured from basket bottles and loud heavy metal music (his favorite) could always be heard.

My mother occasionally gave him food and all the change she could spare. This was how he was able to scrape together an existence as a part-time student at the Faculty of Law at the university there. After a while, he also rode a real BMW motorbike. It was an old model R60 that he was able to maintain all by himself.

The motorbike had been stolen years ago and later found in one of Utrecht's many canals. Witnesses had seen a white, slim man in his fifties push it into the water late at night. But then again, this was not a very good description of the suspect, Bram had told us.

He had stood listening to this story and it seemed like he was a bit relieved, but I had paid no further attention.

After the motorbike, Bram only drove cars – first, second-hand cars, and then increasingly newer models. But now that he was employed by a law firm, he had access to a brand new company car, a small, black BMW.

In the afternoon Bram came to pick me up and together we went for a ride. I eagerly sniffed the smell of new leather when I got in beside him. 'What a great car. How fast can it actually go?'

'Ah, you know, I do like it,' said Bram, 'but I just don't really like cars that much. In fact, I still long for my motorbike.'

Nevertheless, we spent a pleasant afternoon cruising along the motorway – first in the Netherlands, and then also a bit on the German *Autobahn*, to see how fast we could go. Extremely fast, it turned out.

Later that afternoon, we ate a sandwich at a roadside restaurant, overlooking the car park, where the new car attracted glances from men walking admiringly around it.

April 1978 – A new car

He received an exceptionally good car expense allowance, which he could also boost by claiming for more kilometers than he actually drove on business. Privately, this allowed him to drive for nothing, or practically nothing. And what was even better, he could regularly buy another car to match his job.

His first car was a second-hand Volkswagen Beetle. The pictures in the family photo album show Mum and the children smartly dressed in Sunday clothes. They're ready for the weekend car ride, and their faces look serious. The little boy is wearing a grey teddy jacket and the little girl has a red woolen cap on her head, which of course looks grey on the black-and-white pictures from that time. Mummy is posing in the doorway and has a fussy scarf around her head, on which is draped an incredibly large Grace Kelly bun. He is not in the picture, as he obviously had to take the photo.

The Beetle was traded in for an old Citroën Ami, with those crazy wings above the rear window with the indicators in them. The Ami was then traded in for a Peugeot of slightly more hip trim, although that too was second-hand.

One of his heart's desires was to own a brand new car. And after much procrastination and a clever trick with the tax return, a brand new, shiny car appeared in front of the house one fine day. It was a dark blue Alfa Romeo. Ideally, he would have preferred a bright red one, but alas, that would somehow not look right to his customers.

He stood proudly guarding the driveway with the Alfa all day, with neighbors and casual passers-by being treated to haughty looks from him. If a positive comment followed about the car, he smiled affably. He allowed neighbors to inspect the dashboard up close and look under the bonnet. But sitting behind the wheel was only for him.

But that still wasn't enough attention for his car. After all, he felt his status had risen now that he was going through life as a new-car owner. So, the whole family hopped into the car to go for a drive. To Grandpa and Grandma's, of course. The children sat on the new back seat in their best clothes and were told to keep their 'dirty fingers' off everywhere.

Arriving at Grandpa and Grandma's house, they received a lukewarm reception, and the vein on his temple began to swell dangerously. He had expected something better, that much was clear.

With a lot of persuasion, he managed to get Grandpa to go for a drive, and in no time he had lit a cigarette and was puffing away lustily. Really enjoying himself, Grandpa proposed a visit to an uncle, who lived in the next village and who also just had a new car. But 'no, that wasn't such a good idea.' In the end, the trip with Grandpa lasted only fifteen minutes.

For the rest of the afternoon, the new car sat in the driveway with the windows down to get rid of the cigarette stench.

Late at night on his way home, he stopped at the cheap petrol pump. He always did, as it easily saved a whole guilder per fill-up, compared to the pump in his own village. But this time he didn't stop to fill up, but to vacuum the car and wipe the dashboard with a wet cloth. The children could not manage to sleep through all this, and ended up standing next to the car with Mum, waiting for him to finish.

29 February, 1988 – Free dinner

He was financially well off. However, in the holiday home where he had moved to live since the divorce, he had adjusted the stove so that it could no longer burn at full blast, which was nice and cheap. But even though it wasn't such a harsh winter, it must have been uncomfortably cold in the long run. Whole days, he sat in the covered shopping center in Apeldoorn, where it was nice and warm. I heard from Mum that Uncle Hans had told her that he often saw him scurrying around there. Uncle Hans then always turned around unseen as quickly as possible, hoping he wouldn't have to talk to him. Uncle Hans had obviously not told him that he and Tom now lived in a flat above that mall.

And since they hadn't been in touch for a while, they assumed he didn't know their new address. But that was a miscalculation.

Tom was born in the leap year 1956, exactly on 29 February. As that date was on the calendar only once every four years, since childhood his family had always organized an extra-large birthday party for him as a kind of compensation for the three previous birthdays when the party had to be celebrated on another date. Hans had adopted the tradition and made sure that there were lots of goodies to eat and drink in the house. He had also invited many friends and family along. At the pastry shop in the mall, where they were regular customers, he had bought boxes full of gourmet snacks, and everything was now displayed as a buffet on the kitchen counter.

That evening, he suddenly appeared in the middle of their living room. He had boldly walked in with invited guests who had come in through the front door. Defiantly, he stood in front of Hans and Tom, ignoring Mum and me. We ducked behind the backs of several of the other guests and waited tensely to see what would happen.

The angry voices barely rose above the party music, but we could see everything. From the inside pocket of his thick winter coat, he took out a bottle. There was no label on it. It had to be one of the bottles he always had filled with wine by a local farmer in Denia for a few pesetas: not very tasty if you drank it straight away, and usually like vinegar by the time he got back to the Netherlands.

Neither Hans nor Tom put out a hand to take the bottle from him, so he put it unasked in the middle of the gift table.

Sweating in his far too thick coat, he glanced around the room smiling. Before he had turned a full circle, his eyes fell on the snacks and drinks on the counter. He took off his coat and spread it on the sofa in front of the fireplace. Then he grabbed a plate, quickly stacked it full of food, and snatched a glass of wine. Tom tugged at his sleeve, but he ignored him. Satisfied, and with a big smile on his face, he sat down with his booty in front of the wood fire, which spread a pleasant, free warmth. Enjoying it, he looked into the hearth and started eating.

'I'm Hans' brother. This is really nice, don't you agree?' he said, his mouth full, to a couple who were also sitting in front of the fire. Large bites disappeared into his mouth as he held his feet out towards the fire. The couple watched in amazement at what was happening.

Hans was in the kitchen sharing his distress with a group of friends. After some discussion, one of the men took a now-empty box from the pastry shop, which was sitting on top of the fridge, and began filling it with snacks from the buffet. When the box was full, he nodded his head to the other men. Without a word being exchanged, they walked towards the fireplace like synchronized swimmers.

Once there, Hans kindly asked him if he would just follow them. He could not stand up to such *force majeure* and with gentle coaxing they managed to get him along. In the corridor, they handed him his coat, pushed the pastry box into his hands, and slammed the door behind him.

He neither banged on the door nor pressed the bell for a long time, as I had expected. He probably thought Hans or Tom was standing behind it. But his eyes bored into my right eye, as I watched him through the peephole. Slowly, he moved the pastry box to his left arm. Then his right hand went up. With his index finger, he drew a line from right to left under his chin. Then he turned and walked towards the stairs.

May 1978 – Nice and cheap

On their way to his holiday homes in Spain, later passing by the hovels in France, they always went to fill up the car in Luxembourg. It was cheap there, of course; that was the primary reason. Then they would drive on in one go along winding B-roads, so they could avoid toll roads. Also, it was nice and cheap. It didn't bother him that the journey took so much longer than necessary.

After a few of those trips, he got into the habit of 'stopping for a while' on the outskirts of Luxembourg City. There he would walk into a branch of the *Banque de Luxembourg*. Of course, he didn't tell them what he was going to do there, but it probably wasn't withdrawing money, because he always said during the holidays that he didn't have much money in his pocket. The rest of the family had to wait in the car, no matter how hot and boring it was or how long it took.

After the divorce, Mum told her children that she had received virtually nothing during the division of their joint property. Of course, only joint assets that the tax authorities knew about were part of that division. And according to her, there had to have been a lot of black money, too. After the debacle with the preserve jars in the crawl space, he had come up with a safer storage for everything. And that was in Luxembourg.

Mum had not received any of the things he had deposited in Luxembourg over time. One year after the divorce, she made a bold move and drove to Luxembourg with a friend to make inquiries. But she got zero response: Luxembourg had banking secrecy, and she did not have an account with the *Banque de Luxembourg.* Whether her ex-husband did have one, *non, non, non,* of course they could not tell her that, *madame.* Although the bank employee who spoke to her seemed to have some sympathy for her, the woman could not be swayed and Mum had to return to the Netherlands empty-handed.

4 March, 1988 – Enough is enough

The weather was bleak and gloomy. There was a major NS disruption, and train services had come to a complete standstill. I thought about the phone call I had just received. He had called me to tell me that he was in a new relationship. He sounded unusually friendly and relaxed and asked whether I felt like having tea and eating some tasty snacks together in Diemen. He was sure I'd like his lady friend, but he would not reveal more now. Since the trains were not running, he could pick me up and give me a lift.

I thought quickly. Curiosity finally won out over suspicion, and I asked him when he would be with me. I had half an hour. In that half hour, I called Edgar to tell him I was going with him in the car to meet the new girlfriend.

'Are you up to it, dear?' he asked anxiously. 'Call me immediately if you can, please. To let me know how you are. I'll pick you up if necessary.'

He had intended to keep me in suspense for a while longer, but he was bursting with happiness and pride, so it just escaped him.

'Fenna really is a nice girl, you know.' He stared intently down the road at the headlights. Snowflakes swirled down, making it seem lighter than usual at this time.

'SHE'S A NICE GIRL!' he shouted.

I was dumbfounded. Fenna?

'Yes, I heard you.'

'Well, then. Don't be difficult, I'm allowed to enjoy feminine beauty, right?'

'She's thirty years younger than you, and you just got divorced. And are you only interested in her body, or does the rest of her person also matter a bit, too?'

'Stop it. I haven't experienced anything exciting with your mother for a long time, and Fenna is having a great time with me, too.'

'Yes, for now.'

After a long silence, he turned his gaze away from the road and looked at me from the side for a few seconds. 'You stupid cow, you're just as bad as your mother.'

He had just looked at me too long. Suddenly, the car made a strange, sideways movement, and we ended up half on the verge. He tried to brake, but this caused the car to suddenly shoot back into the road on the left. A split second later, I crashed face-first into the dashboard.

At first it seemed like it was dead quiet, but after a few moments, I heard everything: tapping sounds of metal cooling; the wind blowing through the car; a seagull screaming; and moans next to me. I wiped my chin and saw that my hand was completely covered in blood. Yet, nothing hurt. Everything seemed numb.

'Please, help me,' I heard him whisper.

He was lying in a strange position between the steering wheel and his seat. His right hand was pressed against his neck and he looked at me with big, startled eyes.

'Show me,' I said, pulling his hand away slightly. Immediately, a huge jet of blood spurted through the car, partly over me. I sank back in my own chair and closed my eyes.

Moments later, I heard a car slow down and stop on the verge. Other cars continued slowly on the right lane. Those ones didn't stop.

'Do something,' he said, pleadingly.

We exchanged a glance, and during that glance it became clear to me that I had to do something now, COULD do something now. He saw it, too.

'Show me again.' I pulled his fingers loose from his neck and, with some effort, I managed to pull his hand away. Even now, there was a lot of blood. Pulsating, bright red blood. He tried to push me away with his left hand, but that was impossible from the place where he hung in the car. I lay across him and clasped his right hand against my chest.

Shouts sounded behind my back: 'Hang on, I'm coming to help you!'

I ignored them and tried to bore my eyes into his without blinking. As each second passed, it took me less strength to restrain his right hand. The pulsing also seemed to diminish, and the look in his eyes became more and more incredulous.

Footsteps ran towards the car and the door was tugged. Still, I held his right hand; I pressed my left hand firmly on his mouth. Only when the door opened did I let go. His hand slipped limply from my right hand, which I immediately pressed on the hole in his neck.

The motorist leaned over me and almost immediately flinched.

'Aaaah, what a lot of blood.' A woman stood behind the man with her hands in front of her mouth and eyes like saucers, watching what was happening. She was mumbling something. It sounded like she was praying.

'Um, yes. Could you call an ambulance as soon as possible via the talking post?'

'Sure, baby,' the motorist gestured to the woman.

'May the Lord Jesus keep us,' she cried, and then I heard her running away.

'Are you hurt, too?'

'I don't know, I don't feel anything.'

The man sat next to me in the doorway and said, 'You're doing fine. Just keep pressing. And don't be afraid, I'll stay with you.'

He had a sweet face, which tried to look at me reassuringly. It only half succeeded. From the corner of his eye, of course, he could see what I was seeing. That he was lying limply against the left door with his eyes closed, my hand against his bloodied neck.

After an eternity, sirens sounded in the distance. First came a police car that parked across the road. Then came an ambulance. Just one. He was shoved into the back with an impressive bandage around his neck and an IV needle in his arm. He didn't move. I was placed next to the driver with a large towel on my lap to catch the blood that was still flowing from my nose. With sirens blaring, we raced to the AMC university hospital in Amsterdam. Strange that they were still going to this trouble. Surely, he was dead, wasn't he? Or nearly so anyway?

In the emergency room, my broken nose was set. I don't remember much about it, but I do remember I kept asking how he was. They tried to reassure me: 'He's in good hands here, we're doing our best, and you should have faith that he will be fine.'

Hours later, as I sat upright on the stretcher with an impressive plaster splint on my nose, drinking lukewarm tea from a paper cup, they were still trying to cheer me up.

When it had already got dark, two policemen came by. They wanted to take a statement, so I was wary. I told them it had been slippery on the icy road and that somehow we had gone off the road. No, there had been no other car. But there had been a lot of blood. It had all happened fast. Occasionally, I had to close my eyes for a moment.

Vaguely, I remember the eldest cop patting my hand paternally and saying that I was a hero, had done everything I could, and that it was now up to the doctors to heal my father. As if he were sick.

The nurse sent them off after fifteen minutes. 'This young lady needs to recover a bit. Would you please leave now?'

Thank goodness, they did. I slumped back on the stretcher and closed my eyes again.

One of the officers said, 'If you feel better, will you come by the station to complete and sign your statement? There's no rush, though; next week is fine. You can call for an appointment. I'll put my business card here for you.'

A few hours later, I woke up with a jolt. Someone had taken off my shoes and put a thin blanket over me. Light was already shining through the window. My whole face throbbing and throbbing, I couldn't breathe through my nose, and I could barely get my eyes open.

Cautiously, I tried to sit up.

The nurse who had been with me before had apparently seen me moving and came running immediately. She pushed me back onto the stretcher. 'Just keep lying down, dear. There will be a bed for you in neurology soon. We'll keep you here for a while for observation.'

'That's really not necessary, though. If you have a painkiller for me, I can go home.'

'We'll have none that. You can't. Let me just ask how your father is.' Five minutes later, she came back and said cheerfully, 'He's not conscious yet and he's lost a lot of blood, but he's doing reasonably well given the circumstances. Maybe he'll start to recover tomorrow and then you can visit him for a while. We are really doing our best for him.

'I'll take you to neurology now. We will clean you up a bit there, and you'll also be in time for a meal. If the doctor agrees, you may be allowed to go home as early as tonight.'

Struggling was futile. I just had to do as she said.

At the end of the afternoon, the doctor came to see me. I was just having a nice dream, which had made me forget about the pain. In my dream, I saw my mother's face. She gently stroked my head, kissed my forehead, and whispered, 'Don't worry, baby, enough is enough. Sssshhh, sleep tight.'

But the doctor suddenly pulled up one of my eyelids and shone a light in my eyes. I woke up with a start, and the pain pounded through my face again.

He took a good look at me from a distance. 'We straightened your nose again as best we could. But a second time, it usually doesn't succeed as nicely as the first. By the looks of it, the first time was only a short while ago, heh? A hockey mishap, maybe?'

Hockey? 'Um, yes,' I said, trying not to disagree with him.

'Well, you'll come for a checkup in a week, then we'll see how it has worked out this time. The nurse will give you painkillers in a moment. Get well soon.' The medical students who stood behind him immediately followed him towards the exit of the room. They didn't even give me a second glance.

And here was the nurse again. 'How will you get home? Can you call someone?'

Stupidly, I hadn't thought about that for a moment. 'Yes, I would like to call my brother, I'm sure he could pick me up.'

'Just get dressed then. Your things are in that plastic bag on the chair over there. When you're ready, come to the office at the end of the corridor on the right. You can use the phone there for a short call. Can you manage, or should I help you get dressed?' There was no need.

After the call, I waited patiently for my brother. I had left my blood-stained coat in the plastic bag. I had no other coat, otherwise I would rather have thrown it away.

June 1978 – Blood

Mum wasn't afraid of blood. She was a nurse, and therefore used to it. She briskly brushed away blood, washed stained clothes, and put bandages on her children's knees.

But when her daughter had gotten the handlebars of her scooter in her face while scootering up instead of down the kerb, she was shocked at how dirty the girl's clothes were. She had put them in a bucket of soapy water to soak, hoping they could still be saved.

After two weeks, when one of the girl's front teeth discolored blue-gray, mum carefully inspected everything and decided to visit the dentist. The girl had never visited there before, and she had been looking forward to an exciting outing. But before she could say anything in protest, the dentist had her in a hold and, like an executioner, pried open her mouth with his big hands. With a huge pair of pliers, firmly and in one jerk, he pulled the tooth out of her mouth. And again, there was blood. But now Mum was there in time with a large handkerchief.

On the way back home, Mum praised the girl for not crying and said, 'Women can stand blood much better than men, dear. That's because we menstruate and have children. If men had to endure all that, the world's population would halve. At least.'

Her little daughter was too young to understand all that Mummy was saying but felt honored she was being spoken to by her mother like a real big girl.

What it meant to menstruate, she discovered a few weeks later. After the cramps in her tummy, there was – seemingly without cause – suddenly blood in her panties. And quite a bit, too. The panic she felt increased rather than decreased after Mum explained to her that she was now a real woman.

5 March, 1988 – Escape

Bram stormed into the hospital corridor where I was sitting and ran straight past me towards the nurses' station. There, he knocked politely on the door. I half rose from my chair, but he was already inside. Five minutes later, he came out with the nurse. She waved at me for a moment, shook my brother's hand, and then disappeared through a door which had a red lamp burning above it.

I had always loved my brother, but now I was so relieved to see him that I immediately started crying terribly hard. He was clearly shocked when he saw my face. 'You look awful, I didn't even recognize you. I'm sorry. Are you all right?'

Carefully, he sat down on the chair next to me and put his arm around me. 'Hey, take it easy, you're still alive. Will you come to Utrecht with me? There's nothing we can do here now. No visitors are allowed in the ICU after six o'clock.'

So, he was in the ICU.

With my plastic bag, my pockets full of painkillers, and a horribly swollen face with a plaster splint stuck to my forehead and nose in the shape of a large T, I walked towards freedom holding Bram's hand. With gentle coercion, he pushed me under a red blanket into the back seat of his BMW, got behind the wheel himself, and drove towards Utrecht. Every now and then he looked in the rearview mirror to see if I had stayed neatly lying down on the backseat. After more than half an hour, we stopped in front of the house where he had been renting half a floor for a few years. There he helped me up the stairs and tucked me into his neatly made bed.

'Do you want something to eat?' he asked.

'No, but I'd love a cup of tea.'

He nodded and turned to the kitchenette to start making a large pot of tea. Strong and hot, with a big splash of milk, that's how we both liked our tea best. Holding two mugs, he put mine on the bedside table and sat down on the chair with his own one. He looked at me thoughtfully. 'Shall we call Mum, or wait until tomorrow?'

Oh no, I had completely forgotten about that.

'Yes, do, or it will be too strange, even if they are no longer together.'

Bram walked to the hall where a large Bakelite phone hung. I heard him dial my mother's number. But after a while, without saying anything, he placed the receiver back on the hook.

'No answer,' he shouted. Just as he was about to walk back into the room, the phone rang. 'Ah, she's already returning the call herself.'

But she wasn't. It was someone from the AMC hospital to say that our father had sadly passed away at a quarter past twelve. 'Sorry for your loss.'

May 1979 – Chickens instead of a dog

The children watched all the popular children's programs on the telly: Fabeltjeskrant, Pipo the clown, and Swiebertje. Flipper and Lassie replaced them as they got older. The girl fantasized that she would have a dog she could play with for days, which would always watch over her just like Lassie, and that she would love to pet. But no matter how much she begged for one for years, no dog was allowed even for a minute in the house. Mum thought it was too dirty, he too dangerous.

A few months ago, though, there were suddenly three little chicks in the house. Mum had brought them from the local supermarket just before Easter, in a cake box. Just in time, as it turned out, because animal protection services did not think it was a good idea for everyone to be able to pick up a chick with half a dozen eggs.

The girl had watched the chicks with fascination for days, on her knees in front of the box. Her brother felt too big and tough for that and did not participate in the fun, although he had occasionally looked longingly at the critters whenever his sister picked one up and cuddled it.

But unfortunately, the chicks were soon too big for the house. When one escaped and pooped all over the room, Mum had taken them to Grandpa and Grandma's the next weekend. They had a large chicken run in the garden, and there the chicks grew into big roosters. From then on, when they visited Grandma and Grandpa, the children would always check on the roosters first.

After a few months, he came to have a look, too. He wriggled through the small door of the chicken run and grabbed the largest rooster by its neck. Drilling his eyes into the girl's, he slowly twisted the thrashing beast's neck. When the thrashing was over, he crawled out through the little door and gave the now limp rooster to the boy.

'Go and take it to Grandma!' When the boy flinched, he said to him, 'It's dead. Hurry up, go.'

As the boy reluctantly walked away with the dead rooster stretched out in front of him as far as possible, his sister pushed her fingers even harder into her ears and squeezed her eyes shut, so as not to witness any further of her chicken's demise. She heard him snort contemptuously as he walked past her. And she and her brother had to eat the chicken soup, even though Mum had said they didn't have to.

March 7, 1988 – *The funeral director*

That Sunday, the three of us stood together in the corridor in front of the mortuary door. My mother nervously picked at the buttons of her coat. My brother hummed softly to himself until he realized this might be inappropriate and abruptly stopped and cleared his throat. And I stared at my shoes.

Together, we were waiting for one of the AMC hospital staff to open the door for us. It took a long time, and it didn't smell pleasant in there – like disinfectant or something.

I didn't feel well and the plasters on my face were itching nastily. 'Don't pick at them, darling' my mother said, patting my head softly.

From around the corner came the clink of a large bunch of keys. A small woman, almost a girl still, came towards us. Her blonde ponytail swayed happily back and forth to the beat of her brisk little steps. She offered us her condolences and then opened the door. We stepped inside a kind of waiting room with low chairs and tables with boxes of tissues on them.

'Please, wait here a minute,' the girl said, disappearing through a red door at the back of the room. Again, that swaying ponytail.

My mother slumped on a chair and kept repeating, 'Incredible, don't you think?' It really was not a question, it just sounded like she was still surprised. And then she shook her head. She looked neat, but had forgotten to put on lipstick. Normally she would never have shown her head outside the door like this. She ignored my brother and me; she had enough on her mind.

After a few minutes, the door to the corridor opened again, and an elderly gentleman in a black suit entered. Without further explanation, it was immediately clear that he was the funeral director. He walked up to my mother, pressed her hand professionally, and condoled with her great loss. Then he pressed Bram's hand and mine. Because of his accent, it was sometimes difficult to understand everything else he said all at once, but maybe we were also just a bit vague all together. Still, it was clear that he expected us to say goodbye to the corpse together. Yikes. I was not going to do that!

So, I waited in one of the low chairs while my mother disappeared through the red door on my brother's arm. They stayed away for a few minutes, then they joined me at the low table.

My mother insisted on a quick cremation. When Bram and I looked at her in surprise, she said, 'Cremation is so much more hygienic than burial, isn't it? And I just don't feel like waiting for days for a funeral. Remember when Grandpa died, we didn't like that at all, that funeral. I'd just rather it was all over this week.'

I was surprised but kept quiet. I didn't really care much. I saw that Bram had his reservations but did not want to argue about it now either.

The funeral director cleared his throat. 'It should be possible on Saturday, but we need to have received the necessary paperwork from the municipal coroner no later than tomorrow or the day after, otherwise we will run into problems with scheduling and sending out the invitations.' Seeing that we didn't understand him, he told us a little more.

'Only in case of a natural death, the attending physician may her or himself issue a death certificate and give leave for burial or cremation. But death after a car accident is a non-natural death by law. And in these cases, the municipal coroner, after usually only a summary investigation and inspecting the remains, has to issue a burial order. He's already done his job, as far as I'm aware, but it just always takes a little longer to receive the necessary paperwork.'

I felt goosebumps all over my body. My mother apparently didn't like it either. She looked steadily at the tips of her shoes and repeated that she just wanted to get it over with quickly, all of it.

'I don't foresee any problems,' the funeral director reassured her.

And although she was divorced from him and she had little say in the matter, we decided together with the funeral director on the right coffin, flowers, and on whether there would be coffee and cake and a support car, and whether we wanted a priest, pastor, or imam to attend. We opted for a private ceremony without a religious service. We did not order flowers. We told the funeral director he would have wanted it that way.

But the real reason, of course, was that there were no friends or relatives who would want to come anyway. My brother's girlfriend Annet, whom my father had always hated, didn't want to come on principle. And we wanted to keep religious matters out of it, as we were non-believers. The Surinamese funeral director showed little reaction, and he assured us that he would take good care of our father. He gave us the address of the crematorium in the far western suburb of Amsterdam where we would meet that Saturday.

June 1980 – Flowers

He didn't like flowers. They were useless and far too expensive. He liked buttercups in the garden, but you couldn't pick those. Tulips were going to hang anyway, and mixed floral arrangements were always a mess, so not worth the money. Once, when he had pricked himself on the thorn of a rose handed to him by a PvdA-party campaign worker just before the elections, he thought those were rotten flowers, too. So, on principle, he never bought any.

But sometimes he made an exception. For instance, when Mum was sad. And then, by way of a grand gesture, he produced a huge bouquet from behind his back when he came home in the evening. He always wanted to please Mum, right?

She always took these bouquets with a shy smile and arranged them in a beautiful vase, which was displayed in the middle of the dining table for at least a week. And of course, he then also got a kiss from her.

On the night he had given his prettiest bouquet ever to Mum, Grandpa died. After being told the news by his eldest brother, he had put the phone down, shocked, and explained to Mum what had happened. She said he should go to Grandma's at once, to support her. She would stay home with the children.

'Hold on,' she said, as he prepared to step out of the door. In the kitchen, she took the bouquet from the vase and cleverly wrapped it in brown paper, then pressed it into his hands to give to his mother for comfort and consolation.

'Are you out of your mind?' he asked her. 'Bouquets are for festive occasions. The man just died, do you think it's a celebration?' The flowers disappeared into the bin.

He arranged the funeral along with his brothers. It was a chilly event, somewhere in a windy churchyard in the Eastern Achterhoek region. The vicar looked on in dismay as the family said goodbye at the grave, without him even being allowed to speak a comforting word or read a scripture. And there were no bouquets – just one white rose on the coffin in defiance. From Grandma.

8 March, 1988 – Statement

The following day, the same police officers I had seen at the hospital took my statement. They asked me to tell them in my own words what had happened. I tried to stick as closely to the advice Annet had given me, and so I told the truth – at least, the part I had also told her and Bram. Her business card (Annet van Rijn, Master at Law, Buergher & De Wyth, De Bilt) was in my pocket.

So, I started explaining that my parents had divorced last year and that I had had a somewhat difficult relationship with him. That I was surprised when he called me (I didn't say 'pleasantly surprised') saying that he wanted to introduce me to his new girlfriend and wondered if I would like to meet her. I told them that I was curious, and set off with him in the car to meet her. No, I had no idea who she was; he hadn't told me yet when we suddenly got into a skid. And after that, everything had happened very quickly. I especially remembered all the blood, my hand on his neck where it had spurted out. Nothing else really, except that it hadn't ended well for him. And that we had said goodbye to him last week.

The elder of the two officers typed my statement on a pre-printed form. His typing was laborious, with only two fingers. Clack, clack, clack, on an old Olivetti typewriter. For a moment, I considered offering to do it quickly myself, but I bit my tongue.

When he had finally finished, he put the form on the table in front of me, asked me to read it carefully and then, if everything was correct, I had to sign on the dotted line at the bottom.

Afterwards, he pressed my hand and wished me a speedy recovery. He also wished me strength in this difficult period. My statement was clear and matched with those of the witness, the police officers at the scene, and the ambulance personnel. And since it was a one-sided accident and the driver had died, in all likelihood this would be the end of police investigations. I had behaved bravely, both immediately after the accident and now, the police officer told me.

The youngest police officer walked me to the exit. Just as he pressed my hand, the nice policewoman from two years ago entered. Ria, I remembered. In a flash, she recognized me, too, despite the plaster splint on my nose.

'My word, such bad luck again.' Pondering, she took me in from head to toe, then she was off. She quickly arranged her nicely decorated uniform jacket neatly over her back. I stayed behind in the corridor.

May 1982 – *The inexplicable*

'You shouldn't try to explain the inexplicable. You have to accept it, otherwise you'll lose your mind,' Mum used to say. The children didn't understand any of this. It sounded enigmatic, like an incantation formula. As they got older, they found that it started to sound more and more like a doomsday menace, meant to stop any further discussion. Especially if that discussion was about why she stayed with him.

'Simply because I love him, and because I feel sorry for him,' she would say. And this was again followed by her saying, even when she saw in the looks of her children that they didn't understand.

The girl would start at university and be independent in a year and a half; the boy had been just that for some time. Now was the time for action, according to the boy. Quite happily, the girl would look for a job to support herself and would study part-time if necessary. Mum didn't have to stay with him for her sake either. But no, Mum was implacable. She stayed with him.

'Are you afraid of being alone, maybe?' the boy asked. No, it wasn't that.

'Don't even think we won't see you again,' the girl said. She would never think that either.

When the children ambushed her with an appointment with a social worker who could help her initiate divorce proceedings, she was angry. Terribly angry. It was her marriage, and she wasn't leaving him. Full stop.

10 March, 1988 – Punched on the nose

On Thursday morning, precisely at ten o'clock, I reported to the front desk of the ENT clinic at the AMC hospital. I was fervently hoping that today I would be freed from the plaster splint on my nose, and that what came out from under it wouldn't look too bad. I had never been a pretty child (he always called me 'his ugly duckling' to other people, and then he'd laugh a little) and a crooked nose wouldn't make things any better. I had by no means yet turned into a swan.

In the waiting room was a motley collection of people flicking through old magazines. Everyone carefully avoided looking at each other, me included. So, I had no idea why everyone was there and hoped against my better judgment that they wouldn't see my ugly nasal splint. I quickly counted heads. Seventeen people in total. It was going to be a long wait, that much was clear.

On the low table in the middle were yesterday's newspapers, tattered periodicals, and very old books. The only book left was a Donald Duck comic book. Nice. I sat on my chair and started to read the comics. Chip and Dale snacked from Della's biscuit tin. Huey, Dewey, and Louie went to the swimming pool. And Scrooge McDuck did the breast crawl through his piled-up money. Utterly delighted, I was totally absorbed until my sleeve was gently tugged.

I was startled and lowered the book. An older woman pointed to the Donald Duck comic book and whispered, 'Can my granddaughter have a look at that book? She has to wait a while and maybe it will distract her a bit. She's quite nervous, you know.' The girl on her lap looked at me expectantly with a shy, harelip-skewed smile.

'Of course, please,' I said, and handed the book to her. I got an even bigger smile.

I smiled back at her from under my weird plaster splint.

'Ms De Wit!'

I jumped. 'Yes, I'm here,' I said, half standing up and looking at the lady behind the counter.

'You may enter treatment room 3. The doctor will join you in a moment.'

Treatment room 3 was a chilly little room with a large white chair in the middle, which most resembled a dentist's chair. Other than that, there was only a stool on wheels to sit on and a chest of drawers with a shiny metal tray on top. Since the dentist's chair somehow didn't seem all that appealing to me, I sat down on the stool.

Again, I had to wait a long time. Out of sheer boredom, I rode around the room in circles on the stool. I pushed off with my feet and skidded around the dentist's chair, going faster and faster, until finally I hit the chest of drawers with a bang.

Behind me, the handle of the door went down. When the door opened, I had already turned around and looked innocently at whoever was entering. It was a female doctor with four pimply medical students in her wake.

She looked at my records, which she had been carrying under her arm.

'Ms De Wit?' she asked.

When I confirmed that I was, she asked me to sit on the dentist's chair, then she sat down on the stool, right in front of me.

'How do you feel now a week's passed?' she asked me. 'Any pain? Can you breathe a little through your nose again? And how did sleeping go?'

Before I could answer all those questions, she started picking at the plasters used to stick the splint on my face. 'I'm sorry, this might hurt a little, but we're going to relieve you of this nasty thing,' she said.

'What should we look for in nasal trauma?' she asked the medical students.

'Um, for fractures, and for possible dislocation of the septum, maybe?' said one of them.

'Hmmm, yes, that's a good start.'

Now that I had been relieved of the splint, she used a kind of metal pinch to open my nostrils one by one to look inside my nose as well.

'Just removing an ugly scab, you know,' she said. 'It won't hurt, because I'll apply some numbing drops first.' She was actually quite a sweet person.

She opened one of the bottles in the drawer cabinet and put some liquid on a small cotton ball, which she pushed up my right nostril with tweezers. It tickled, but as promised, it didn't hurt. Not even when she used those tweezers to pick something out of my nose. Then she thoroughly inspected the insides of both nostrils once more. What she saw obviously pleased her.

She asked if the medical students could have a look as well. They could; I didn't dare say no.

After some back and forth talk between her and the students, she sat on the stool, giving me another good look. It almost made me shy.

'Fortunately, it turned out quite beautifully. A stroke of luck for you, I'd say. I read in your papers that you broke your nose once before in a hockey accident, so my colleague did a really good job. It may well be that your nose looks better now than before. It is nicely straight, and your septum, which is the bony bit in your nose, is also neatly centered again. Once the hematomas have subsided, you will be very pleased with the result. Just be careful for a few more weeks, and don't play hockey, because it will take a while for the fracture to heal properly.' She smiled kindly at me.

I thanked her warmly, relieved that I would be walking out the door without the splint. I also thanked the medical students, although I don't really remember why. Then I left the ENT department.

In the waiting room, I waved to the girl with the Donald Duck comic book, but she didn't notice.

In the main reception hall of the hospital, I walked past the toilets, and I decided to take a pee before boarding the underground again. When I looked in the mirror above the sink, I was shocked. Around my still puffy eyes, there were dark circles. I looked like a raccoon. Even with that horrible splint on my face, I would have looked better.

I bought a small roll of mints in the hospital shop. The girl behind the till was apparently used to quite some nasty sights, because she didn't flinch when she saw my face. I slipped the roll of mints into my coat pocket, along with the big sunglasses with red frames I'd just snatched from the rack.

Outside the hospital's revolving doors, I carefully put the sunglasses on my nose. Now I could go home relatively unnoticed.

June 1982 – Anesthetic

There was a cut on the girl's eyebrow, and the swelling had left the wound open. Something had to be done about it, because this wouldn't mend itself, she realized when she inspected it carefully in the mirror in the bathroom. Mum wasn't home yet, so she couldn't ask her for help. It was inevitable that she would need to go to the doctor's surgery by herself, before school started.

After a short bike ride, she stepped into the waiting room with lead in her shoes. There, she sat down on one of the wooden chairs with her schoolbag on her lap. She occasionally dabbed the plaster on her eyebrow with a paper tissue. It leaked through.

After half an hour, it was her turn. She was the last patient; the surgery hours were almost over.

The GP looked at her kindly from behind his desk. 'Well, from that big patch over your eye, I can guess what you're here for,' he said. 'Have you fallen down again?' He walked around his desk and began peeling off the plaster. 'Oy, that's an ugly cut, indeed. We'll have to stitch that up a bit, otherwise you'll have an ugly scar. And our young lady obviously wants to look her best, huh?' he said, patting the girl's cheek paternally.

He turned to his desk and, through the intercom, asked his assistant to come in to help with a minor procedure. He winked at the girl and murmured, 'It will be done in no time, you know, my little beauty.'

From a chest of drawers, he started to put things onto a metal tray – small packets, some kind of scissors, and tweezers.

When his assistant was inside, they stood together in front of the girl to take a good look at how they could close the wound as nicely as possible. The GP, with his back to the girl, did something over the tray. His assistant stood next to him and laid some bandages, plasters, a small bottle, and a sterile-packed syringe next to the other stuff. Then she wiped over the wound with a cotton ball soaked in disinfectant.

When the GP turned around, he had a curved needle and thread in his left hand and scissors in the right.

'Just grit your teeth, please. We'll do it without anesthetic, because the anesthetic prick is worse than a few stitches.'

Over the girl's head, the assistant looked startled at the doctor. But he just shook his head in warning, and immediately afterwards he pricked the girl's eyebrow with the curved needle. And again, and again, and again. It hurt. After the fourth prick, the girl felt no more pain. A faint nausea moved up from her stomach, and she felt she had to vomit... then nothing. She woke up on the stretcher.

'You fainted,' the assistant said, handing her a cup of water.

She drank it down slowly. Wobbly, she sat up straight and, with a little help from the assistant, climbed down and sat back on the chair in front of the doctor's desk. Her jumper reeked of sweat and vomit. The doctor was no longer in the room.

'You'll need to catch your breath. I must go back to the front desk to answer the phone,' the assistant said. 'But sit tight now. I'll come and check on you in a minute, and then you can go home.'

After a few minutes, the girl saw everything in focus again. How much longer would she have to sit here? She saw that the small bottle was still on the tray in front of her. It contained lidocaine, she read on the label.

She quickly looked around and put the bottle, the still-wrapped syringe, and one of the packets of ready-made suture, in her pocket. Then she crept down the hallway and left the surgery.

She could not go to school in that state, so she would need to go home and put on a clean jumper first.

She put her loot under Mum's pillow. Then she got back on her bike and rode to school, where she lined up with the other latecomers to get a note from the janitor. For punishment, she had to sweep the schoolyard in the afternoon.

All day, she didn't say anything. But even without words, Mum understood who had put the presents under her pillow.

12 March, 1988 – Cremation

Early that Saturday morning, we stood at the entrance to Westgaarde crematorium, waiting for the hearse. It was cold, and the wind cut through my far too thin coat. Shit, I should have worn my red woolen jumper. You wouldn't have seen any of the red color under my coat anyway.

What kept them? Bram went to stand in front of me to catch the wind.

Just then, the hearse was slowly coming up the path. The funeral director walked in front of the car with a top hat on and a solemn look on his face. Behind us, the doors opened, and two employees of the crematorium came out with a kind of stretcher on wheels.

When the hearse had come to a halt in front of the steps, they slid the coffin onto the stretcher. Then they laid an ugly wreath on the lid. One of its green ribbons read in gold letters: *'For the best husband and father'*; and on the other: *'Kisses from Judith, Bram, and Kiki.'* Damn, she had done that without consulting us. Why on earth?

The coffin was placed at the front of the smallest auditorium they had. There were about twenty chairs ready, but we only needed three. My mother quickly looked around to see if anyone would enter, but of course there was no-one.

When we were seated, all was quiet for a while, and the funeral director seemed to be waiting for other guests. When it took too long, Bram gestured that it was fine and we could start.

The funeral director closed the auditorium door and disappeared behind a curtain. There he put on the first piece of music. It was a piece of hard rock music that Bram had selected from *So far, so good, so what,* by Megadeth. I was surprised, but grinned at Bram. How he would have hated this music. He had always forbidden Bram to listen to 'such awful noise'.

The next piece of music was one I had chosen, and it was a traditionally appropriate one for a cremation ceremony. Even the funeral director seemed to appreciate it, looking relieved. It was Allegri's *Miserere Mei*. I enjoyed the thin voices of the boys' choir, which sounded beautiful in the auditorium. Thanks to the divinity classes I had had at school, I found the lyrics comforting. For a moment, I forgot why I was sitting there. But after about five minutes, all was quiet again.

Bram and I had declined to speak, and the funeral director had nodded understandingly. 'Yes, it's always difficult to speak at a funeral or cremation ceremony,' he had said. But my mother had insisted on doing just that.

I was curious to see if she would shock the funeral director with a nice little anecdote about our beloved deceased. She stood up and smoothed the now crumpled paper in her hand against her coat.

'We agreed that I would address you,' she read from the note.

'Huh, is she going to speak to him now that he's dead?' I thought. 'Yuck, what's the point of that?'

'But I don't really know what to say,' she continued. 'I'd love to hear your voice again.' She sighed deeply. Suddenly, the coffin sank into the depths, towards the cremation oven, because time was running out.

She left the rest of the text on the paper unread, and quickly sat back down.

August 1982 – Fortune teller

Her brother had promised the girl that he would take her to the village fair, so she was looking forward to the outing and eager to look at all the rides. Since they were all very expensive, she assumed that she would be limited to looking only. With her pocket money, she would treat them to candy floss or a cinnamon stick. He could choose between these two favorites.

Together, they set off. Smeared with the sticky remnants of candy floss, they watched with great interest what was going on at the fair. Their trek ended at a red tent from which incense swirled and Oriental music sounded. A sign above the entrance, which was closed off with a curtain, read:

Madame Rose will consult with the dead on your behalf. The world's most reliable fortune-telling!

'Come,' said the boy. 'We're going to this fortune-teller; I'll pay for this. Let's see if we have a bright future ahead of us.'

The girl grinned delightedly, and a moment later they were sitting at the table in the tent with the fortune-teller. She looked exotic in a brightly colored dress with glitter, black-rimmed eyes, a big black wig, and giant earrings.

At first, she ignored them and stared, as if in a trance, into the large crystal ball that stood on the table in front of them. This went on for a long time, and the silence was uncomfortable. Jeez, if this was it...

But suddenly the woman said to the crystal ball, *'Oui, mon cher. Oui, moi aussi.'* The children were quite startled.

Then Madame raised her eyes to heaven and moaned, 'Oooooh, come to us. Are you there? Can you give me your message?' Apparently, the spirits also spoke plain Dutch.

Somewhere from under the table, there was a loud bang. Brother and sister sprang up, but the fortune-teller didn't react and she remained sitting at the table, groaning loudly, wiggling her upper body. In a strange voice, she started emitting strange noises. It was eerie and also fascinating. The incense fumes hung heavier and heavier over the table.

Then suddenly she clawed at the boy's left hand and the girl's right hand. 'I sense that there is happiness and sorrow in the future for you.' Her eyes bored into the girl's. 'I sense you are going to travel a lot.' Then she looked at the boy. 'Success, I see, and love.' She concluded with a whisper, 'But beware, fate is lurking and may catch you off guard.'

Laughing, they rolled out of the tent. When they walked past it again half an hour later, the fortune teller was sitting next to the tent with an older man, talking animatedly and eating chips from a paper bag. Her wig was on the table next to the bag.

11 March, 1988 – Observation

Since we had decided that we would walk to the café, we had to brave the cold. Had I known it would be this cold, I would definitely have insisted on a taxi. There we were in our black clothes, ploughing against the wind.

My mother wanted an arm from my brother. Musing, she said, 'I got nothing in the divorce, he made sure of that. But you will lack nothing from now on.'

Bram cast me a warning glance. She continued, 'Those houses will fetch quite a bit, I think. Now there's a piece of luck from this... um... this event.'

I still hadn't taken off the sunglasses. From behind the dark lenses, I observed my mother. Actually, she looked very good, much better than before, despite the fact that she was a diabetic and had been injecting herself with insulin three times a day for several months. What was it exactly: freedom? Would she ever go out with another man, or would she stick to her female friends? I wished her a wild, sizzling fling.

She was definitely attractive, so she wouldn't have to put too much effort into interesting a man. If only she could let go of that plaintive, self-centered tone from earlier. I said nothing, just looked from one to the other and kept walking.

'Yes sorry, dears. It's not about that at all. I just need to get used to the fact that he's really dead. Sorry,' I heard my mother mutter.

I thought about my own anger at the time, about my frustration that she had stayed with him for so long, despite the terrible marriage in which she had been a prisoner. And that even now – as it turned out – she was not really capable of seeing her own role in all that had happened, other than as a victim. But to be fair, she had been a victim, just as much as my brother and me. And all three of us were also complicit in our own pasts, somehow. Me, too. Or had we just been cowards? Obediently, we had always done what was required of us, and we had all kept our mouths shut to the outside world. They hadn't realized what was going on. Or they didn't want to know.

We walked towards the café where we had ordered a coffee table for ourselves and a number of people who came to pay their respects. When we stepped inside, Annet was already waiting for us. She had brought Bram and me to the crematorium in her big, leased car. My father had never been able to stand her, so she had declined to be at his funeral and had gone straight to the café to wait for us there.

She kissed Bram first, then me, and finally, a little awkwardly, my mother. 'How did it go?' she asked no one in particular.

Bram replied, 'It went smoothly. And nice that you can have it over with in just under fifteen minutes, with some music and a speech. Just the way he would have wanted it.'

The minimum time for renting the auditorium had been fifteen minutes. For me that had been exactly fifteen minutes too long, and I was relieved to be sitting here now.

Bram looked at me questioningly. 'Are you all right?'

My mother, who thought he had asked her, said dreamily once again, 'Yes, who could have thought of that...?' She said she hoped there would be something to eat soon, otherwise her blood sugar would get too low.

After a while, the room filled up with old acquaintances of my parents, whom we had only seen occasionally. Uncle Hans also came in with his partner Tom. He was obviously startled by my battered face but said nothing about it. Uncomfortably, they stood next to my mother. Since there was little talk, the bowls of vegetable soup and croquettes came in handy. And the drinks served afterwards loosened tongues a little.

My mother, after downing a few dry sherries, had bright red cheeks and responded eagerly to my uncle's question if she wanted a ride back home with him and Tom. Yes, she wanted that very much. She seemed relieved that it was over.

She stood up and, without turning back to us again, she allowed Uncle Hans to help her into her coat. Holding his arm, she stepped out through the big revolving doors.

At the same turn of the door, Edgar stepped inside. He had to get used to the dark for a while, then he saw me sitting at the table. He walked over to me, didn't say anything at first, but just held me tightly for a while.

'I was too late at the crematorium, otherwise I would have given you a lift,' he whispered in my ear. 'I thought you could use a little company from a friend. Greetje had to stay with Junior, but she told me to wish you strength.'

Then he held me at arm's length and took a good look at my battered face. 'Oy, that doesn't look too good.'

I was so happy to see a friendly face that I immediately found myself grinning, I couldn't help it.

'This is Edgar,' I said to my brother. 'You saw him in the hospital in Apeldoorn last year, remember?'

Bram smiled broadly and said to Edgar, 'If I can believe half of what Kiki told me about you, you are an exceptionally good friend to her. Thank you for everything.' The men shook hands, then Annet was hugged enthusiastically by Edgar.

Together, we sat out the time. Most of the guests left after an hour. A number of others, strangers to us, were having a good time together and were clearly intending to stick around. We did not. When the croquettes and soup were finished, we stepped out through the revolving doors to freedom.

November 1983 – Hide and seek

His eldest brother had hated him from the first day he was in his cot. At first, he was just jealous that the mutt got all the attention and Grandma suddenly had no time for him. But in the years that followed, he turned out to be a really nasty, selfish little boy, who never once did anything for someone else without benefiting himself, was always cheating, didn't shy away from cruelty to the animals in the yard, and could raise a terrible throat if he didn't get his way. Grandpa and Grandma were routinely terrorized by him; they were just a little afraid of him. And the vague notion of fear didn't diminish as he got older.

So, everyone was happy when, thank God, he left for Australia shortly after his marriage.

'Good riddance,' thought the brother wickedly, as the ship pulled away from the quay and he was able to comfort Grandma. She was sobbing with relief next to him, saying, 'I'll never see him again.'

So, it was a nasty surprise when the young family suddenly showed back up at Grandpa and Grandma's four years later. But the children who came along were delightful, and his sister-in-law was truly enchanting. They had initially moved in with Grandpa and Grandma, but fortunately that hadn't lasted too long. Grandma loved having the grandchildren with her, but he didn't appear to have changed a bit, and he was still bossing everyone around. The one did not outweigh the other, and Grandma was soon close to a nervous breakdown. Besides, the household jar was also quite empty.

He had been taken aside by his eldest brother, who had given him an ultimatum: he and his family had to find their own accommodation or pay a hefty board to Grandpa and Grandma. Why had they been shacking up there for free for so long, when – if the stories were to be believed – they had earned good money? If something didn't change soon, the following weekend the issue would be discussed with the whole family!

He had no choice but to arrange housing for his own family as soon as possible. He didn't want to pay board, and he couldn't stand up to the whole family at once, especially if it was suggested to him that he must have earned piles of money in Australia.

When they left for their own flat, Grandpa and Grandma breathed a sigh of relief. The brother was also relieved at first. But in the years that followed, he increasingly noticed his menacing looks and the anxious features of his sister-in-law and children.

'This is not OK,' he often thought.

Just after his nephew fled the house, the uncle noticed that his sister-in-law had a big bruise on her upper arm. He pointed at it and whispered, 'Him again?'

She said nothing, but just looked startled. Her daughter, standing next to her, nodded emphatically. The uncle hugged Mum and whispered something in her ear. Then he ran to the garden, where his brother was polishing his car.

'I'll beat you to death, stone cold, as dead as a doornail, you hear, if you ever do that again!' he shouted at him. 'You son of a bitch.'

'What do you mean?' he asked, twisting the polishing rag around his fist. 'Are you all right, you PANSY? Well, go on, hit me then, if you dare,' and he remained defiantly facing his brother.

The uncle walked down the garden path, his face flushed in anger, and tears of frustration in his eyes.

12 March, 1988 – The inheritance

At eight o'clock in the morning on Sunday, Bram and I stood together on the muddy forest path that led to the holiday cottage where he had lived until last week. It was just getting a little light, and the other houses further down the forest path became visible through the trees. It looked gloomy and neglected, and there were deep potholes in the path where a car would easily get stuck.

'We have to be careful,' said Bram. 'Basically, we accept the inheritance if we step over the threshold and take something with us. It's all or nothing when it comes to inheritances. So, it's better if no one sees us.'

I blindly trusted my brother on this point – as on all other points, for that matter. During his part-time job at the notary's office where he worked as a student, he had often heard about how things could go wrong when drawing up wills and settling inheritances. I had also heard many a juicy story from him about this. Arguing widows, children, and grandchildren, who had to fight among themselves about who would get what. There had even been someone who had read his will himself and had it recorded on VHS. So, from the television, he spoke to his summoned relatives after his death and told them in no uncertain terms that they would inherit nothing, that everything would go to charity. It was amazing indeed what people could think of to bother their family even after death.

'OK, what do you suggest?' I asked.

'We're going inside, but won't turn on the lights yet. First, we're going to collect that suitcase in the basement. Then we'll have a quick look around to see if there are any things we would like to take with us. I would like to have some children's photos, Annet would like to see them, too. Other than that, I don't need anything else. And I'm sure you'd like to pick up something he nicked during the divorce. Then we'll be off.'

He took a key from his pocket and stuck it in the lock. I was surprised he had a key, and it probably showed on my face.

'Mum's,' Bram said. 'She always had it, but she didn't dare come over here to pick up some stuff, so she has given it to me. I did dare, but I didn't feel like it.' He grimaced at that.

Well then, we didn't have to break in, which was fine with me. By touch we found the door to the smallest bedroom, where the entrance was to the big cellar. The hatch was jammed a little, but together we lifted it and walked backwards down the steep stairs, one after the other.

Arriving downstairs, Bram pressed the light switch on the wall to the right. Two fluorescent lights flickered on. We stood in a huge room with large shelving units along the wall. It seemed bigger here than the original holiday home above ground.

'Pass me that treasure map,' Bram said.

I grinned at what was a good joke. 'Here,' I said, pulling it out of my pocket. 'Read it aloud again.'

He raised his eyebrows sarcastically, then unfolded the paper and read the letter in a sarcastic tone.

Apeldoorn, 30 August, 1987

To my dearest Kiki and Bram,

I've always tried my best to be a good father to you. You two have never been able to appreciate that. Marriage with your mother was very difficult for the last 10 years. And you took sides with your mother, always blaming me. I've always found that was terribly unfair.

After all, I always sacrificed myself for you and always did what was best for all of us! In doing so, I made a significant contribution to your education, laying an excellent foundation for great careers. With interest and full of pride, I follow your progress as much as possible.

I have not been able to pursue my own ideals, because you did not approve of me taking over the business, afraid that you would then also have to roll up your sleeves. Never, ever, could I count on you. In itself I would not have minded sacrificing my own ideals to you two. But having to experience your ingratitude over and over again, I am sad to say I made the wrong choices. It is as if my life has failed. If I could do it all over again, I might not have cared what you all said about my own plans for the future. I would have been the proud owner of a thriving company by now, I'm sure.

I was less and less able to find human warmth with your mother, so I looked for that elsewhere. I'm not proud of that, but please try and understand it a bit.

Now I don't know what to do anymore.

I wish you both all the best. You seem to be mad at me, but I am not at you, though a little gratitude would have been nice.

Should you come to my house after my death, please take a look at the bottom of this letter. Near the cross I marked, you will find a black suitcase. In it are some things I no longer need. Do something nice with it; I cannot do so myself anymore. A thank you will also be missing this time, but it would not have reached me anyway.

Your loving father

Underneath it, he had drawn a map of the basement with a ballpoint pen, with a cross marked in the back left corner. A treasure map indeed, ha-ha.

I couldn't help but snort disdainfully. So he wrote that the day before his staged suicide. Must have taken him all day, to write that letter.

'Ridiculous... pompous somehow, but not really. The stupid jerk,' Bram said.

He stuffed the letter in his pocket and walked to the corner. At the bottom of the shelving unit, he tried to move the half-empty paint cans apart, but it was not easy. Everything was stuck together with spilled paint, and the handles of the cans were hooking together. When we eventually managed it together, there was indeed a black suitcase behind the paint cans. Bram lugged it upstairs, with me at his heels.

'Heavy. What could it contain?'

He tried to shake the thing to hear what was inside, but it was too heavy for that. And unfortunately, the locks were closed, and we couldn't find a key. Even using a knife from the kitchen drawer, we did not succeed in getting the case open.

Since we didn't want to stay in the cottage for too long, we decided that we should keep our curiosity at bay for a while. A quick look out of the windows convinced us that everyone in the other cottages was still asleep, but surely that wouldn't last long. We had to be gone before anyone saw us.

The photo albums had to be in the stuffy living room, but in my haste I couldn't find them. Too bad. I did see a framed photo of my brother and me hanging on the wall. I tucked it under my arm and was about to walk out with Bram when I saw a litter bin to the right of the front door, bulging with rubbish. Another glance and I saw what it was: children's drawings, school reports, swimming diplomas, ribbons from annual four-days walking events, traffic diplomas, the whole lot. Everything expertly torn and destroyed.

I tipped the entire contents onto the floor in the middle of the room, looking for anything intact. A few pages he had torn from the photo albums were still in one piece, and some photos had survived, including a few childhood ones of Bram and me. I handed them to my brother. 'Here, take them for Annet.'

As my brother drove, I sat stoically beside him with the heavy suitcase on my lap. After a while, we stopped at a roadside restaurant where we ate a hearty breakfast in silence among the truckers. Bram ate a ton of eggs with bacon, and I ate three sandwiches, double-topped with butter, ham and cheese and mustard. We washed everything down with big cups of steaming coffee, as though we were starving from the hard work.

The suitcase stood between our feet under the table. Every now and then I secretly felt with my foot to check it was still there, but I avoided looking at it.

I kept my sunglasses on the whole time, because I didn't feel like being asked about my black eyes by the truck drivers at the other tables. I'd rather they thought I was a poser. From behind the dark glasses, I kept a close eye on them. No one would be able to get to the suitcase without fighting a little battle with me, I imagined.

When we had emptied our plates and Bram had carefully looked around to make sure no one was listening, he asked, 'Are you coming to Utrecht with me first?'

I had actually thought that Bram would drive me straight to my student flat, but I'm not exactly sure why. He looked at me with raised eyebrows. 'Let's check together and see… um… how many photos and such we have.' With his head, he gestured in the direction of the suitcase.

I chewed on the biscuit that had been with the coffee, understanding what he meant. 'All right,' I said with my mouth full.

Again, in silence, we drove to Utrecht. In his room, Bram carefully placed the suitcase on his bed. After some fiddling with a screwdriver, he managed to break open the locks and the lid opened.

The suitcase was packed full of neat rows of colorful banknotes from all kinds of countries. I saw German

Marks, US Dollars, British Pounds, Dutch Guilders, Australian Dollars, and several rows of currencies I had never seen before. Stunned, we looked at the contents of the suitcase. Bram whistled softly, as if to let a beautiful woman know he appreciated her looks.

I cautiously picked up a stack of red twenty-five Guilder notes. 'How much would this be?'

Around the stack, which was about as thick as a large desk diary, was a faded paper band which read *Banque de Luxembourg*.

'Golly, I wasn't expecting this,' my brother said.

It was well past noon by the time we had examined everything. Using the list of exchange rates from last weekend's *Volkskrant* newspaper, a big calculator, and a notepad, we made a rough estimate of the value of all the banknotes. It proved to be quite a job. But in the end, we calculated that the total value must be somewhere between three hundred and three hundred and fifty grand in guilders.

Among the stacks of banknotes were also sixteen Krugerrands, each individually wrapped in a kind of Plexiglas case with numbers on it, and a gold embossed stamp. We had no idea what these would be worth.

And at the very bottom, under the Krugerrands, we found a crumpled yellowed envelope containing our, now also yellowed, original birth certificates from Australia.

Speechless, we looked at each other then sat side by side on the bed, our backs to the suitcase. It took a long time before Bram was the first to move. He carefully examined the birth certificates then pinned his to his notice board. Then he put mine back in the envelope and handed it to me.

'I've asked him for that thing several goddamn times. The prick. Now I can finally stop trying to get one sent to me from Port Augusta.'

I didn't understand what this was all about, but didn't question him.

'I think you take some of the Dutch notes with you to Amsterdam for a start,' Bram said. 'Then you can pay everything you need in the coming months and just finish your studies. We'll have to get rid of those Krugerrands. I don't want that South African apartheid shit. Do you?'

No.

'Here, take this.' He picked up a stack of twenty-five-guilder notes. I put one of the notes in my purse. The rest I stuffed into my bra. The birth certificate went into my left jacket pocket. In the right one was the photo frame with the childhood photo of Bram and me.

Tired, we drove to Amsterdam in his car. There was still not much talk on the way. After some pondering, my brother said, 'What you do is up to you, but I will reject my share of the inheritance. I don't want anything to do with his shady dealings. That pile of money in the suitcase is crazy enough for me.' Good plan, relief. I was going to do just that, too!

March 1984 – Birth certificate

The son now lived on his own and had a sweet girlfriend with whom he would grow old. Although he was not very impressed with the institution called marriage, he was eager to oblige her. Nor did he necessarily have anything against getting married, either. If that's what it would take, he would gladly sign a deed during an archaic ceremony, in which he would in effect promise to take good care of her. He intended to do that without any deed anyway. He had known that from the first day he had met her.

And he was going to do it all very differently from what he had experienced at home as a child. His only condition was that the ceremony itself would be small and short, and it would be followed by a big, informal party with friends. She, in turn, was fine with that, of course.

They wanted it to happen right after graduation. If they were both studying solidly, it could all be in about a year. And they could save up for the big party in the meantime.

No sooner said than done, they went to the town hall to get their marriage license. At first, the official was very friendly and congratulated them on their intention. She started filling in the details. Everything was going well until she asked the young man where he was born. Suddenly she was not so friendly.

No, if he'd been born in Australia, he'd have a problem. After all, there were so many sham marriages with Ghanaians and such who acquired Dutch citizenship by marrying a Dutchman. To prevent this, there was a policy that anyone who was born abroad and who wanted to marry a Dutch citizen, had to submit an original birth certificate. If necessary, the marriage candidate could also request a copy of the birth certificate in his or her country of birth, but it had to be authenticated by the Dutch Embassy in that country and be not older than three months at the time of the betrothal.

She didn't care that the post took weeks and that the young man had no family or friends in Australia who could mediate. In that case he would simply have to go there himself to arrange it or something. It was not the city's problem, but that of the suitors in question – of the young man, in this case. 'Equal treatment in similar cases,' said the official, because the city did not want to discriminate at all.

The intended bride said that her boyfriend was not a similar case at all. After all, his parents were Dutch. Therefore, under the Dutch Citizenship Act, he had had Dutch citizenship from birth, so this was all nonsense, really. He had just shown her his Dutch passport, hadn't he? But the official didn't want to listen to this. And good afternoon, if they would just leave now, thank you very much.

On the steps of the town hall, the young woman cried bitter tears. Her boyfriend tried to console her and, with renewed resolve, despite his reluctance, decided to ask his father for his original birth certificate.

But the latter immediately made it clear that he would only hand over the certificate if he was promised that he would be invited to the wedding. And the boy would not promise him that sincerely enough. So, the marriage was postponed indefinitely.

4 March, 1989 – Moving house

A year of ever-increasing relaxation had passed. I studied a bit, still worked part-time at the Municipal Insurance Department, often babysat Junior, regularly went to my dinner clubs, and on the weekends I usually went to Utrecht. Thus, everything quietly rippled on.

Through Edgar, I had been able to rent a small studio in Czaar Peterstraat. It was a bit of a dirty old shack, but after a weekend of scrubbing and cleaning, it was a palace. I took over the stove, the boiler, three ceiling lights, a gas cooker, and an old fridge from the previous tenant. 'Just give me twenty-five guilders for it,' he had said. I thought it was a good deal and quickly handed him the banknote. He was probably glad that he didn't have to carry the old stuff down all the stairs.

Some of the Spotty Nibblers had lent me a hand with cleaning and a lick of paint here and there, and we had a fun time together. Bram and Annet had helped with wallpapering. And my mother had come for a day to thoroughly scrub the tiny bathroom on all fours. She had looked at the fridge disdainfully then disinfected it with chlorine in every nook and cranny and behind every rubber strip. The thing stood proudly gleaming in the kitchen, awaiting fresh food.

When everything was ready, Bram hired a van and, early in the morning, we shoved some boxes of my belongings into it. I put the key to my room in the caretaker's cubby hole. I didn't see him or the students on my floor in the student flat. They all thought I was a stupid bitch, and they were right about that. Goodbye. Personally, I wouldn't miss them either.

Arriving in Czaar Peterstraat, Bram parked the van askew on the pavement. With a hoist and block, he lifted the boxes to the third floor. And I tackled them from the open window. Within an hour, we had finished the job.

Standing among the boxes, we drank coffee from the thermos flask that Bram had brought with him. He looked around pensively. 'Still a little bare, huh? I hadn't realized you don't have any furniture.'

'No, I rented that room furnished.'

'But how long did you think you could sleep on that air mattress?'

I shrugged. 'Dunno.'

He looked at his watch. 'I still have some time. That van doesn't have to be back at the rental company until four o'clock. Shall we drive to Ikea in Bijlmermeer to pick out some stuff for you? I'll give you a bed as a present.'

I thought this was a great idea. Quickly, I pulled some of the banknotes out of a boot I had hidden them in. I wanted to buy something nice myself, something new! I had never done anything like it before, and I had not seen the inside of Ikea either.

In the big blue store, Bram bought me a Murphy bed and desk combo. For the first time in my life, I saw exactly what this was. What a nifty thing, indeed! It would fit nicely in the alcove in my studio apartment, and then I would have a desk right there. I bought the office chair myself. And after some procrastination, I found ready-made curtains with rods, a large bulletin board, and a 'starter set' for the kitchen, with pots and pans, cutlery, and a 24-piece crockery set of brightly colored pottery.

At the till, I saw some more colorful trinkets for a few guilders. On a whim, I also put those on the belt. I watched them move forward with satisfaction, ready to be scanned by the cashier who blew happy pink gum bubbles.

Once I stood at the till myself, I broke out in a sweat. Bram paid for the Murphy bed and desk combo and got a large paper receipt with which to collect it in the store's basement. And I had to pay almost a hundred guilders for the other stuff. I had never paid such a large amount.

The girl behind the cash register didn't look up, put the banknote in the till, and pressed some change into my trembling hand. To her, it was nothing special. Rather, it seemed to bore her, and she quietly continued to chew on her pink bubblegum.

With my purchases piled up like trophies in the shopping trolley, I patiently waited with Bram at the collection counter in the car park downstairs until the furniture, packed in a number of mysterious flat boxes, was handed over to us. Sitting on a curb in the car park, we shared the hot dog I'd bought with one of my last guilders, just behind the till. We grinned at each other with our mouths full, mustard smeared around our mouths.

The boxes turned out not to fit in the van and were very heavy. Stupidly, we had been too greedy. At the counter, Bram inquired what it would cost to hire a trailer. The price turned out not to be the problem, but the fact that we had not booked one. And Bram wouldn't have time to return the trailer in time either, if we could have got one at all.

After some bickering, one of the guys behind the counter handed my brother a sturdy piece of rope and a wide roll of packing tape. If we left the doors of the van open, it would work, he said. And it did, although it was quite a task to cram everything firmly into the van and tie the doors tightly with the rope and lots of tape.

Grinning, we drove back to Czaar Peterstraat. There it turned out to be a terrible hassle to get the large, heavy packages upstairs. The small packages could go up the stairs. But because it was so narrow, the big ones had to be hoisted. Bram had to brace himself to lift even the smallest one. It took a lot of strength to pull it in through the window, but it all just barely worked. Getting the bigger packages up would require a miracle.

Suddenly, from the corner store, a rather overweight guy ran towards Bram, who was just trying to get the second package up. With a look of understanding towards my brother, he wordlessly grabbed the rope as well. Together, they hoisted everything up without any problems. Then he slapped my brother's shoulder and introduced himself as Siep. 'This is where we help each other, you know. Welcome to our street!' Then he waved cheerfully upwards and walked away at his leisure.

'Will you make it till tomorrow on the air mattress?' asked Bram, inspecting the blisters on his hands. 'Unfortunately, I don't have time to help you put that bed together now. I'll be back tomorrow, promise!'

'No thanks,' I said. 'You go to Annet now. I'll call you tomorrow. I think I can ask one of the Spotty Nibblers to help me. I'll call you. And there's really no hurry.'

With gentle coercion, and after kissing him, I worked him out the door.

'But how can I reach you?' my brother asked as he stood on the small landing.

'I'll arrange a phone connection later this week and then I'll call you right away, I promise!'

'No, call me tomorrow evening anyway, Kiek. Otherwise, I'll be worried.'

I promised.

When he was gone, I walked through my new home, enjoying myself. I took in every nook and cranny. But arriving in the alcove where my bed and desk combo would be, I saw that the air mattress had deflated. Punctured, no doubt. Oh no. It would be hard to sleep on the floor.

But wait. Of course, I could take the mattress from one of the boxes and lie down on that! After a short struggle, I managed to get the mattress out of the box and to strip off the plastic bag it was in. It smelt deliciously new, and with my sleeping bag pulled tightly around me, I went to catch up on some sleep first.

When I woke up to a city bus thundering down the street, it was already dark. Through the windows, which were not yet curtained, I could see people rushing home through the streets. It was raining, and by the looks of it, the wind was also blowing quite hard. I had totally forgotten to buy some food. And I had almost even forgotten the taste of the hot dog I had shared with my brother.

Out of the corner of my eye, I saw someone across the courtyard looking at me. It was an old woman, looking out from her floor on Blankenstraat onto my kitchen on Czaar Peterstraat. Resting her arms on the windowsill, she was watching everything I was doing. Long, gray hair peaked around her head. For a moment, I flinched. But when she suddenly smiled broadly at me with her wrinkled face and almost timidly waved at me, I pulled myself together. I waved back and was treated to an even wider smile. She pushed up her kitchen window and gestured to say something to me. With some effort, I also pried up my kitchen window.

'Hello, are you coming to live here?' she asked.

'Um, yes, indeed. My name is Kiki. Today my brother helped me bring my stuff here.'

She nodded approvingly.

I thought for a moment. 'Do you know perhaps if there is still a supermarket open here?'

'My dear child, Siep's night shop is right on the corner of your street. You can go there right now, it's open. By the way, my name is Sjaan. Nice to meet you, dear. Good luck with everything,' she said sweetly.

Moments later, I was in the evening shop.

'Hello there, neighbor, all's well?' asked Siep.

'Um, yes, all things are upstairs, but I still have to unpack and hang curtains and stuff. Let's have some food first, I thought.'

'Yes, that sounds like a good idea. Has your boyfriend left already?'

'That was my brother, Bram. He has gone back to Utrecht.'

I piled some food in my basket and felt Siep following me with his gaze the whole time. Yet, it wasn't annoying. He was very friendly. Like a fat teddy bear, he occasionally winked at me with his beady eyes.

At the till, Siep asked cautiously, 'Have you got someone to help you out with those curtains?'

'Um, yes, my brother is coming again later this week and he will help me with that.'

There was silence for a moment, and then Siep said, 'It is entirely up to you, but my stepson has a small handyman business. He is a bit special; slightly autistic, you should know. But if you want, he'll hang those curtains for you in no time.' He saw my hesitation. 'I don't want to force anything on you, and I understand that, as a girl, you have to watch out for yourself, but he's really sweet, you don't have to be afraid of him. If he does something he shouldn't do, I'll break his legs.' But the latter didn't sound threatening. He gave me a kindly questioning look.

So, before I knew it, I was in the room with Johnny. He had carried in a kind of leather shopping bag, completely filled with all kinds of tools, nails, screws, glue, and paint. Without hesitation, and without even looking at me, he set to work.

Within half an hour the curtains were neatly hung in front of the windows. He then skillfully screwed the Murphy bed together and assembled the desk under it. It was ready within an hour and a half. I was impressed.

'Thank you, Johnny, I'm so happy about that,' I told him. 'How much do I owe you?'

'Settle up with Daddy Siep, please,' he whispered.

For a moment he looked up, but he didn't really look at me, rather gazed at my chin. A shy smile crossed his face, then he stormed down the stairs.

Papa Siep, of course, didn't want me to pay for the job. It was his welcome present, and he would arrange it with Johnny. 'Just come and do your shopping with me from time to time, then I'll be more than happy.'

That evening, I ate homemade macaroni from a new Ikea plate. I sat on my office chair, with my back against the wall and my feet towards the stove. And I was very satisfied.

After dinner, I counted the money I had left in the boot. It was over three hundred guilders. One of the paper bands from the *Banque de Luxembourg* was still around the pile. I considered spending the money on some more furniture. Would it be enough? Or should I just wait and see if I could manage financially, without having to knock on Bram's door for a new pile? I preferred not to, as we had agreed that we would not throw money around so that we would not attract attention.

In the end, it was not necessary to spend a lot of money on furniture. Once a month, Siep had Johnny inspect the bulky piles of rubbish which could be put on the pavement on Monday morning by anyone in the city. His harvest consisted of three kitchen chairs, a dining table, two armchairs, a bookcase, and a small coffee table. He spent hours repairing and refurbishing them. And he covered everything with a fresh coat of new paint.

In six months, my furniture was complete, and it looked great. It had what they now call a vintage look. As agreed with Daddy Siep, I always paid Johnny a modest amount for his services. Much more importantly, I occasionally had a chat with him and Johnny in the corner shop. And I sometimes helped them write and neatly type out official letters to the municipality, the tax authorities, or to suppliers. If colleagues had odd jobs that needed doing, I always gave them Daddy Siep's number, and Johnny would go there with his tool bag.

At Sjaan, I would wave every now and then. She always waved back enthusiastically. Sometimes we exchanged a few words through our kitchen windows. At Christmas, she gave me a homemade card, and I brought her some apple beignets on New Year's Eve.

It was, in short, a successful move.

24 April, 1984 – Permanent residence

Over the years, he had expanded his first holiday home with his own hands so that it would be suitable for permanent residence. He hadn't said anything to Mum, but he had planned to move there when he retired. Then the house he lived in now could be rented out and generate nice extra income.

He had built a porch and then glazed it, and had added ceramic floor tiles. He had also dug a large cellar. Without planning permission, of course; he refused to pay for such a thing. And the morons from the municipality never came to inspect anyway, so he could go about his business as he damn well chose. By now, it was no longer a tiny cottage, but almost a real house.

He did need some help, though, to replace the still leaky roof. After much urging and cajoling, his brothers agreed to help him for a day, and his daughter, of course, went along to take care of the sandwiches and coffee. She shouldn't complain that she couldn't just go away for a whole day during the weekend so close to her final exams. She would pass anyway, and she could bring a textbook with her if necessary.

To save costs, he scoured building sites, looking for leftover batches of suitable beams, insulation material, gutters, and roofing sheets. In the end, he found everything he needed with his own employer. The man was only too happy to get rid of a batch of gray corrugated sheets that had been sitting in the corner of the warehouse for over ten years. He was even allowed to take them for free. And they added a few wooden beams, just to please him.

Today, all the building materials were delivered. The men stood, cups of coffee in hand, biting into sandwiches, watching as the lorry drove up the muddy path, then everything was hoisted onto a large pallet in front of the cottage.

The youngest brother, who worked in construction, pulled the plastic off the pallet and looked suspiciously at the corrugated sheets. 'Those aren't asbestos sheets, are they?' he asked him.

'Oh, don't worry so much. Do you really think they still use that?'

After some grumbling, they set to work.

As quickly as possible, the roof was repaired with everything that was on the pallet. The girl had to stay inside the cold cottage for safety reasons, but all the hammering, sawing, and banging was driving her crazy. She couldn't concentrate on her school books, and could only hope that the work would be finished soon and she could go home.

30 June, 1989 – Graduation

In the end, I had passed all my exams and only had to write a thesis. Instead of attending lectures, I spent almost every morning in the university library on Singel. I dreamed away a bit, with a large stack of reference books in front of me on the table. Occasionally, I wrote something down. There was no need to hurry, as far as I was concerned.

Sometimes, I would just sit and do nothing for a while. Then I would study my fellow students.

When I had almost finished the thesis, and I was once again dreaming away in the university library, I suddenly noticed someone making eye contact diagonally across the large table. I was startled. It was Wieger, and he had signaled that he wanted to talk to me, outside, now.

'Well, well, so you suddenly left. How are you?'

'I'm fine, thank you. If all goes well, I'll graduate at the end of this month. But what do you really want?' I had asked him. 'We weren't exactly friends, so say what you have to say, otherwise I'll go back inside.'

He had his eyes half-closes and had come to stand right in front of me. 'OK, then, we won't pretend we're friends. I just wanted to ask you to tell your dad to give Fenna a call. She hasn't heard from him in a long time. And actually, I think that's outrageous.'

I did not get a chance to ask or say anything.

But at the modest drinks that the University of Amsterdam offered me and my fellow students today on the occasion of our graduations, an uninvited guest suddenly appeared in the doorway. Or two, actually. It was Fenna and her baby, a girl of about six months old.

Fenna walked purposefully towards me and just looked at me sternly.

'Congratulations on your degree,' she said. 'I can't stay long or Roberta will start crying. I brought you the card because I didn't know your new address. Here you go.'

She pushed an envelope into my hands, turned, and left, without speaking to anyone else.

'Who was that?' my mother asked. 'Didn't she want a drink, or couldn't she stay because of the baby? Such a young mother, but gorgeous, though. And such a beautiful baby. Just as much white hair as you and Bram had when you were little.'

I opened the envelope in the evening when I was safely home, my heart pounding. It contained a birthday card with colored balloons and pre-printed congratulations. She had crossed out the word 'birthday' and written 'degree' in block letters underneath.

Inside the card was her message:

Dear Kiki,

Your father hasn't been in touch for a long time, and I couldn't reach him by phone either. I have since understood that he has changed his mind and no longer wants to marry me. In hindsight, maybe I should have made other choices, but I was naive. He told me about the bad relationship he had with your mother for years and that, once he was divorced, he would definitely marry me. That time you saw us on Leidseplein, it was too early. I got the morning after pill then. But Robert asked me to marry him at the end of February last year. And when I had missed my period for a few weeks and we were celebrating having a baby together, he wanted to tell you and Bram first and ask if you wanted to come to our wedding. Your father had brought all kinds of tasty snacks from an Apeldoorn confectioner to celebrate with you.

Did you not grant him happiness and tried talking him out of it? Did it bother you that I'm the same age as you, Kiki? Is that why I haven't heard from him since?

Please tell him to contact me. I would like to move on with my life, and he hasn't deposited any household money in my account in ages. Maybe, despite everything, he also wants to get to know Roberta.

Fenna de Boer
21 III Kruislaan
Amsterdam
020-662819

13 July, 1984 – Friday the thirteenth

Tense, she waited on the stool by the phone for her headmaster's call. He had promised a call between noon and one to everyone who had passed their final exams, otherwise it would be later. Although she was fairly confident that she had passed, tension ran high as it got later and later. But that turned out to be unnecessary. He called just a few minutes before one and immediately said, 'Passed, of course. Congratulations. I'll put my phone down quickly, because I still have to call someone else, bye.'

Mum served her a large piece of home-baked apple pie and together they celebrated with a small party. With some acrobatics hanging from a bedroom window, they also managed to hang the flag and her school bag on the flagpole. Soon enough, a few neighbors came by with congratulations and flowers. But they quickly disappeared when he got home.

He didn't ask if she had passed; he just assumed she had. 'Look, for you,' he said, placing a blue Giro envelope on the table in front of her. He always used those envelopes to keep things in, because they were nice and free. And apparently there was a present in this one for her now.

'Thank you,' she said politely, opening the envelope.

Out came a blue Giro bank card that had her name on it. There was also a bank statement that showed one hundred guilders had been deposited into the account that very day. A fortune. She was so surprised, she looked at him speechless. This was the best present she had ever received from him. Right?

'Can I pick something myself for that money?' she asked cautiously.

'It's an advance, for when you start studying. To pay for little things. I will pay your tuition fees, train tickets, and books directly. If you need anything else, you can pay for it from this. If you then give me the receipts, I will top it up again.'

'But—'

'I didn't think it was such a good idea for you to move into rooms right away, anyway. It is best to travel back and forth by train. There are no lectures late at night, so there. And I canceled that room. Stay with Mum and me for a while longer.'

1 July, 1989 – Humble pie

Last night, my brother had reacted with shock when I called him late and told him who the girl with the baby was and then read him the text on the card.

'Well, we can add that to the list as well. A half-sister, fathered by a chick who could have been my bloody sister. What a truly disgusting man he was! Wait a minute.'

Apparently, he then held the receiver to his jumper and in a few words was telling Annet what was going on. I heard snatches of what was said and shouted back and forth. Then again loudly and clearly, 'Shit, she doesn't know he's dead!'

'No, that seems pretty clear to me,' I said dryly.

'Let me think for a moment. I'll call you back in a minute.'

An hour later, the phone rang. Much calmer now, Bram said, 'Let's go visit that Fenna together tomorrow. I think she'll be home when she has a little one like that. Then we can tell her together. And with a few of those Krugerrands, we might help her out. Personally, I have no desire for any further contact with her or that child, but let's try to handle it nicely.' It must have been Annet's good influence for him to act like that.

Next morning, Bram and I sat in the car in front of Fenna's door on Kruislaan.

It was a large and stately building, with as many as thirty, all different, doorbells and sloppy nameplates. But even after pressing the right bell a few times, Fenna had not answered. Undecided, we sat in the car and looked down the sunny street.

After a while, the front door suddenly opened and an elderly gentleman stepped out. Yikes, another one of her sugar daddies, no doubt.

'Quick,' said Bram, 'just ask him if Fenna is at home.'

I got on with it. 'Yes, my daughter is downstairs in the basement doing laundry,' the man said. 'She must not have heard the bell. Have you come to see the baby?' His curious, but not unkind gaze had drifted to the small package I held in my hand.

'Um, yes, indeed Mr. De Boer,' I said.

'Well, she'll like that. Since her boyfriend has abandoned her, she has been a bit lonely. I visit every week, but that's not the same as a nice friend coming over.' He winked at me. 'Have fun. Having a nice cup of tea with someone her own age will probably perk her up.' Then he walked to his car and drove off.

I gestured to Bram, and after another few attempts with the bell, Fenna did open. It was obvious that she was startled to see us at the door, but she immediately took a step backwards and walked ahead of us up the stairs to the third floor.

It was a small one-bedroom apartment, about the size of my studio. But this one had a much better finish and nicer furniture, including a cot that clearly had not come from Ikea. With a gesture she invited us to sit on the spotless white designer sofa.

Bram told her briefly and matter-of-factly in a few sentences that waiting would be pointless, because he had died in March last year. I saw no emotion on her face, or at least no sadness.

'How?' she asked.

'It was a car accident. He was cremated on March 12, but we didn't know about you. Nor would we have known how to reach you.'

'And if we had known, we really wouldn't have called you,' I thought viciously, trying to keep a neutral look on my face.

Slowly, a triumphant smile appeared on her face. 'So, he did NOT abandon me! I kept telling my parents that. They kept telling me that Robert wasn't for me, that I should forget about him. And after I had given birth, they urged me to leave it at that. I'm getting an allowance from them now.' Ah, hence the beautiful furniture. 'Just a very small one,' she added quickly after she saw my gaze.

Bram got up and walked over to the cot. He only had to take one look at the sleeping child to see that it was undoubtedly our half-sister. She had unmistakably the same features and the same hair.

'She's called Roberta, after your father,' said Fenna.

'Yes, that's what Kiki said. Look, it's all rather unfortunate. As I said, we knew nothing about it. But maybe he would have arranged something for you if he had been alive. Or at least for the child anyway. That's why we want to give you something we found in his house after his death. You can sell them, and then you can certainly continue for a few years. You can then finish your studies in that time.'

'Oh, sure,' I thought.

Bram gestured for me to give the parcel to Fenna. She almost snatched it from my hand and tore off the brown wrapping paper. Not understanding, she looked at the four Plexiglas covers. She held them close to her nose to see what was printed on them and what was hidden inside.

'They're Krugerrands. Worth a lot. Just ask at Haarlemmerdijk,' I added. Then we left.

Fenna didn't say goodbye and we just closed the door behind us.

December 1984 – In rooms

After a lot of arguing, she managed to move into rooms in Amsterdam after all. She was able to get a room in Casa 400, a 'student hotel' in the Watergraafsmeer district. It was actually an ordinary student flat. But the rooms were rented out with standard hotel furniture, and in the summer months the students had to move out and tourists came in their place. Often these were Japanese tourists who would 'do' Amsterdam in one or two days. Only the top floor was reserved for students who had not managed to temporarily find alternative accommodation or go on a long holiday.

He agreed to the plan that she would move in, on the condition that she would come home every weekend and during the holidays. That way she could collect her household money as well. He would jack up the advance on her Giro bank account a little for unforeseen expenses.

He had calculated that it would also be financially attractive if she moved in here. He would no longer have to pay for train tickets. And in the summer months, there would be no rent to pay. The rent subsidy from the city of Amsterdam was considerable, and she could just drive home and back with him, since he was in Amsterdam often enough anyway.

Indeed, her first summer holiday she was not in Amsterdam and went on holiday with her parents. After that, she decided to take drastic measures to prevent a recurrence.

She told him that there were assignments to be completed, and that she would only pass her exams if she spent every day in the university library. So, she said she had to stay in Amsterdam. Fortunately, her excuse was accepted by him. Mum occasionally called her secretly from the neighbor's phone. She urged her daughter to take good care of herself, so stay away. But all in all, that was difficult with so little money.

26 December, 1988 – Aunt Kiki

I had spent Christmas Day with Bram at Annet's place. Together, we had also celebrated my birthday and feasted on a huge pan of cheese fondue. Rather inebriated, I slept it off on Annet's sofa. In my hand I clutched the box of silver earrings she had given me for my birthday.

On Boxing Day, she and Bram were going to have brunch with some friends in Amsterdam, so they could give me a lift. Of course, I was expected at Edgar, Junior, and Greetje's where we would celebrate my and Junior's birthdays all over again.

At eleven o'clock, I rang the bell. With a big wave, Edgar opened the door and enthusiastically dragged me inside. The table was beautifully set, and everything your heart could desire to feast on was there. Although I had eaten far too much cheese fondue yesterday, I was quite hungry again. It is a miracle that I can always eat so much without getting fat.

Greetje came storming into the room on her big slippers but said nothing. She put her index finger to her lips and whispered conspiratorially, 'He's just sleeping. Be quiet please, so we can eat undisturbed.'

Of course, nothing came of that at all. After only ten minutes or so, Junior began to cry. Uninvited, I walked upstairs and took him out of his cot. He was quiet almost immediately, and because I liked it so much to hold him, I took him downstairs on my arm.

With him on my lap, I sat down at the table and continued eating a little awkwardly with one hand. Satisfied, the little guy hung against my chest and soon fell asleep.

Greetje couldn't resist. 'Would you ever want to have children yourself?' she asked.

'No,' I said gruffly. 'Children are much too nice for that. I wouldn't want to do that to them. And besides, I don't have a husband or boyfriend who can make me have one. Being a single mother does not appeal to me either.'

'First things first, then. Find a nice guy. Then you'll have children soon enough. Maybe we can hook you up.'

'No thanks, Greetje.' And to Edgar, I said, 'Can I have another slice of Christmas bread, please.'

'Hey, let's keep it cozy,' Edgar said. 'And to our son, Kiki will just always be AUNT Kiki. So, we are all one big family, aren't we?'

January 1985 – A suitor

In Denia, where he owned two holiday homes, there were many Dutch people. He had established particularly friendly relations with one couple who met his standards. The man was a fat ex-broker, she a tired housewife who had only one goal in her life: to make her son as comfortable as possible.

That son's name was Jan, and the brother and sister saw at a glance that he had nothing going for him. Of course, he thought they were wrong about this. After all, the son's pale, sulky appearance with hare teeth and chicken breast, stupid interests and absolutely the wrong clothes, were more than made up for by the prospect of a large future inheritance. In short, a good match for the girl.

If only they would behave nicely to him. And those long, brown knee-high socks over his unsavory-looking, milky-white legs, under those far too big shorts, were only practical. That way he wouldn't cut his shins too often on the thorny bushes on the path behind the house, which was the quickest way to the pool.

'Even if he was the last guy in the universe, for God's sake ignore him,' the boy had hissed at his sister in the evening.

She had whispered back, 'Don't worry, I don't like him one bit.'

But during their sparse afternoons at the pool, they were often stuck with Jan. He acted like a jailer. The Spanish boys didn't dare come any closer anymore, and when he appeared to treat them to ice cream, he and Jan had a great time together, so they suddenly found themselves with two guards.

At lunchtime, Jan naturally had a bite to eat with them, smacking and slurping with gusto, and he happily joined in. Initially, the tastiest snacks were always hospitably offered to the intruder by Mum. Later, he simply appropriated them without further ado. On his own, he devoured a large – the only – bunch of grapes for dessert after a (for him at least) copious meal. They watched dumbfounded.

The one time Jan accompanied them on a rare outing, he scolded the waiter for bringing him a glass of orange juice that had too little in it. Then he paid the bill with the money from his wallet, and he was happy for days after because he had left one only peseta as a tip.

The only way to get rid of Jan in the pool was to swim faster than he did. With his skimpy stature, he could usually not keep up with the brother and sister. And that was just as well. If he could unexpectedly get too close, he would pull them by their hair just too long underwater. He almost drowned the boy a few times. And with the girl, he quickly slid his grasping hands along her body. She was disgusted.

When her brother noticed that Jan's hands were going where they didn't belong, he scolded him. Jan was unimpressed at first, knowing he was protected by a powerful man. But after the boy unceremoniously gave him a black eye the next time it happened, he stopped groping the girl in the pool.

Jan's mother remarked loudly during a social evening that she thought the girl was beautiful. Now she was really screwed, she immediately realized.

'Whatever happens, that Jan needs to fuck off. I don't want to see him again.'

'Sure, darling,' said Mum. 'You two are not suited at all. And we are not in Ukibukistan, where fathers arrange marriages for their daughters. Did you hear me?' she said to him, 'I don't want that family over anymore!'

Of course, this ended in a quarrel, as he saw his little plan go up in smoke. But Mum stood firm this time, even though for six weeks he refused to speak a word in front of her and the children. They were no longer that bothered by that. Nice and quiet, right?

But as it turned out, he had stuck to his plan. During his travels through the country, he often visited Jan's parents and schemed with them openly or in covert terms (no one would ever know for sure).

When his daughter had long since left the parental home and spent a weekend at home with her parents, he suddenly called out to her, 'Jan's on the phone for you.'

'I don't know any Jan,' she muttered, letting him press the receiver in her hand.

'How are you?' asked the all too familiar voice on the other side.

'Why, why are you calling?' she asked suspiciously.

'Well, look, I'm studying in Groningen these days. And I thought you might like to drop by sometime...' Silence.

'Why would you think that?'

'Um, and then I have room enough here, so you won't have to go back by train until the next day.'

By now, alarm bells were ringing loudly in her head.

'How did you come up with that idea?'

'Well, just...' he was beginning to sound a bit more uncertain on the other side.

'Just what? For once and for all, Jan, I am NOT coming to Groningen. And should you move, I will not come to you in your new place of residence. I already didn't like you in Denia, and I still don't like you now. GEDDIT?'

'I'm proud of you,' Mum said in the kitchen.

He was too stunned at the time to say anything. Later that afternoon, when she was in the car with him, he told the girl, 'You stupid cow, there's really no one waiting for you. Now you'll grow old lonely.' And then he suddenly gave her a hard poke in the side.

January 1990 – New job

Sometime in January, following my graduation, there were rumors that the Municipal Insurance Department would expand. An International Desk would be set up to deal with the non-Dutch-speaking clients. They could use someone there who knew how claims were handled, could make good calculations, could assess damage reports and who – very importantly – could speak to customers in several languages.

I let slip to anyone who wanted to hear that I had a degree in economics, was fluent in English, and also spoke a fair bit of French and Spanish. Maybe I was saying it to the wrong people, because it didn't lead to immediate results. But I did crave a better position than the poorly paid temp job, now that I was no longer getting a student grant.

Bram and I spent the money from the suitcase sparingly. Otherwise, people might notice. And jobs weren't there for the taking, either. Unemployment had not been this high in years.

Of course, Edgar put in a good word for me. With all my might, I kept my fingers crossed that I would succeed in getting the job. If I had been religious, I would definitely have folded my hands piously, on my knees in front of my bed every night before going to sleep, to beg a divine blessing for the plan. But it took so long to hear anything that I had almost given up hope, when I was suddenly called to come for an interview.

After much back and forth and many job interviews (I remember there were dozens, but I'm sure there were only two or three), I got the coveted job. They thought the fact that I had a university degree looked nice on the business cards, too.

With that, I was immediately freed from the temp agency and entered full-time salaried employment. And with a not exceptionally high, but still nice salary, and a GVB season ticket that allowed me unlimited use of the underground, trams, and city buses, I was overjoyed. A real job! And an indefinite job contract immediately after a three month's probationary period. It was thrilling. Never, no, never, would I just give up this job.

I regularly ate my lunch with the colleagues in my former department – Freek, Jolanda, Marco, and of course Edgar, which was always fun. Furthermore, I saved diligently, hoping to go on nice holiday trips soon. In the evenings, I preferred looking in travel guides to watching television. With almost childlike imagination, I imagined which countries I would visit, that the hotels would look just as nice as in the guides, and that the food would be delicious. Memories of past holidays I simply pushed away.

August 1985 – World tour

During the summer holidays of 1985, the girl travelled to Australia with her parents. 'To see where you and your brother were born,' he had said.

She was 19 at the time and had been studying economics in Amsterdam for a year. But every weekend, and all holidays, she spent at her parents' home. Her brother was 21, studied law in Utrecht, and never came home. He couldn't be forced by him to come along on the trip.

So, the three of them left for Sydney. The plane wasn't fully booked, and they were actually allowed to sit wherever they wanted after a few hours. Delightfully, the girl sat near a window in the Boeing 747, looking outside for hours, a whole row of three seats to herself. Just when it was getting too dark to see anything, he suddenly plopped down on the seat next to her. Nice.

He talked endlessly about his experiences over twenty years before in Australia. It sounded like he had spent years travelling around there on his own and had experienced nothing but great things. Smelling his breath, he'd taken a good sip of the free wine served with every plane meal.

Around her, she saw a number of passengers casting furtive, endearing glances at them: How nice father and daughter were sitting there talking together.

Fortunately, he was also tired, and after half an hour, he left to stretch out on his own row of empty seats in an attempt to get some sleep. The girl also tried to get some sleep and succeeded, despite the noise and her uncomfortable position in the plane seats. She woke up a few hours later because the lights in the cabin came on, and by that time they were already descending.

In Sydney, a camper van would be waiting for them. With it, they would cross the country, heading for where he wanted to go. It would be a little cramped, but the luxury van he had already pointed out in the glossy brochure at home had a small bathroom and a chemical toilet on board, and there was a tiny, separate bedroom for the girl.

She and Mum didn't know that, on second thoughts, he had chosen a cheaper option from another rental company. And that camper van turned out to be a converted truck with a broken gearbox. In the middle of the night, when they had only driven a few hours from the airport, they found themselves stranded with the thing somewhere in the bush.

The much smaller, replacement camper van which was made available by the rental company – after much cursing and swearing – had just enough space for three bunk beds, two of which could be folded up to serve as seats during the day. Everything (cooking, eating, sleeping, washing, and even occasionally peeing in a bucket by the women) had to be done in three meters square. There was, of course, no bathroom or toilet on board. Campsites were not visited; they just parked along the road. That was fine, he thought. Occasionally they could use a toilet at a petrol station to poo, otherwise they had to do it behind a tree. The girl didn't dare, and neither did Mum. And the further they got away from Sydney and towards the desert, there were fewer trees.

They didn't have much water with them, so there wasn't more than a wipe with a washcloth to be had. His request, somewhere in the desert, to be allowed to tap some water into a bucket so they could replenish their supplies, was met with a cautious: 'Depends on the size of the bucket,' from a local.

DUTCH KANGAROO

Sweaty and stinking, they sat together in the far too cramped space, swallowing their chagrin, while according to him they had to drive at least 750 kilometers a day to see everything they (he, that is) were here for.

For long, scorching hot days, they drove between road trains transporting sheep along the narrow tarmac roads through the empty country. Along the road, they saw the occasional kangaroo – usually dead after being run over by passing trucks, very rarely alive. They hardly talked, and avoided looking at each other. As soon as their eyes met, bitter reproaches were exchanged back and forth, and that usually led to prolonged shouting by the evening.

After only a few days, they were sick of each other's proximity, and the girl wanted nothing more than to pack her bags and return to Amsterdam. In the middle of the Nullarbor plain, it came to a horrible clash between them, because he wanted to drive on in the dark while Mum wanted to stop. What the girl wanted didn't matter.

Unfortunately, besides all the money, he also had the plane tickets in a pouch hanging from his neck. Otherwise, the girl would have stopped a passing car on the spot and let herself be whisked away to the nearest airport. This was despite the risk of rape, which he always warned her about if he got wind she wanted to hitchhike. She thought, 'I'll punch him in the mouth if this continues,' but of course she was far too cowardly for that. She knew all too well that he would win when it came to fighting.

With sour looks on their faces, they drove on in silence, towards former neighbors in Port Augusta. Once there, the camper van was parked on the garden path, and they spent a few days there with these very friendly, but elderly people, who were probably happy when they left.

Then they went on to visit the couple's daughter, who was now married to one Sean, who was setting up a vineyard in Western Australia, near Perth. Once there, it turned out that she and her husband had not yet got everything in order. At least, the girl read that assessment in the somewhat disapproving glance her mother cast at their accommodation.

It consisted of three old train carriages arranged in a U-shape. A little further along was an outside toilet, next to the makeshift back door.

Annie saw the girl's eager looks and offered that she could sleep on the sofa in one of the carriages. Before he could intervene, she gratefully accepted the offer. She immediately moved her toilet bag, some clean underwear, and her sleeping bag from the campervan to the train carriage, before he could take her aside to 'dissuade her'.

Four nights in a row, she was delightfully alone. She put the big sliding door of the carriage where she slept firmly on the latch before going to sleep. And during the day she was up before dawn, drank a cup of strong, sweet tea with Annie, swam with her for half an hour in a small lake somewhere down the road, and went exploring. Her parents saw her only in the evenings. Those few days, she really did have a holiday.

Sean wasn't very friendly and clearly hated the visitors. He wanted to discuss anything and everything with those bloody Europeans who made it impossible for him to sell his – not yet even bottled – wine on the European market. The fact that his wine would have to be paid for twice as much as a nice French wine after the expensive transportation, that was not the issue according to Sean. No, it was all due to the import restrictions that he would not be able to sell his superior product in Europe.

Without knowing the details (like about the import restrictions, which the girl had never heard anything about), and with facts that he made up on the spot and attributed to his damned 'statistics', he entered the discussion. He just hadn't counted on Sean being a formidable and fierce opponent in the debate. And, of course, he couldn't silence his host with a slap. Invariably, Annie had to intervene to separate the yapping men.

Three days ahead of schedule, they traveled to yet another new destination. On parting, Annie, Mum, and the girl exchanged emphatic glances. Without saying goodbye to Sean, they got into the camper van.

Their next destination was Bonegilla – the Bonegilla migrant camp where he and Mum had been taken in by the Australian government when they entered the country as immigrants. The girl knew the camp only from the black-and-white photos in her mother's photo album. These pictures showed tiny, wooden huts on stilts, with corrugated iron roofs and small staircases. Her mother had told her that she'd had to work hard in the kitchens in this camp just to earn a bit of pocket money, and that sleeping in the little ovens (because that's what the small houses actually were) had been almost impossible. Why he spoke about it with such nostalgia and insisted on going back to it, was a mystery to her. But he drove very fast with the camper van, as fast as the narrow roads allowed. She tried to make herself small in the back of it, reading a book and looking out of the window, which showed an arid, red landscape with no buildings.

Despite his haste, he only just managed to reach his destination before dark. Once there, it turned out that Bonegilla was no longer a migrant camp, but an army base. Armed soldiers stood at a barrier in front of the entrance. And of course, they didn't raise it. Despite his urgent requests to the guard commander, who was called after much haggling with the soldiers, they were denied entry to the camp. And they were not too kindly requested to drive away and stop blocking access. He was certainly not allowed to take photos of the military complex either.

A few hundred meters away, they stood by the side of the road. Beside them was a high fence with rolls of barbed wire on it. Beyond that lay the unreachable camp. Standing on the roof of the camper van, he tried to catch another glimpse of what his port of arrival in Australia had once been. He couldn't, of course, as it was far too dark by then.

In an icy silence, they drove nearly ten thousand kilometers crisscrossing the country. And on the plane on the way home, she was startled by a friendly steward asking her what she wanted to drink. At home, when asked, she showed the photos and said that the journey had been very impressive.

8 May, 1991 – Wedding vows

Years later than planned, Bram and Annet finally married. At three o'clock in the afternoon, they put their signatures under the deed in the stately town hall in Bilthoven, where they had been living together for a year by then. It was a short ceremony with just the two witnesses (myself and Annet's brother), her parents, and my mother present.

Annet was wearing a tasteful ensemble from a fashion house in Utrecht. And my brother looked good in a dark gray Italian tailored suit, with a tie made of some of Annet's dress' material.

'What a beautiful couple,' my mother kept saying. 'I almost feel like getting married again.'

I wanted to say something unkind, but I didn't want to spoil the atmosphere and my own good mood.

Then we went to the hotel they had hired for that afternoon and evening, where there was a sweet gathering of friends, acquaintances, and colleagues. All were equally enthusiastic, nice and, above all, stunningly normal.

Merrily, everyone served themselves both drinks and snacks from the buffet. In the corner, a nice band played 1960s classics. It sounded good and not too loud. Those who wanted to talk could chat, and those who wanted to dance just did so without any embarrassment. No one had to work the next day (Ascension Day), which also increased the festive spirit.

A professional photographer took pictures. Fortunately, he did so before everyone was slightly tipsy and disheveled. A picture of Annet and Bram, flanked on one side by my mother and me on the other, was my favorite. It still hangs in a nice frame above my desk, next to the frame with the children's photo of Bram and me, and a frame with another group photo: me with Junior on my lap, with Edgar and Greetje standing behind us, waving to the camera, smiling.

30 November, 1985 – Family portrait

In the hall of her parents' house hung a couple of framed photographs. They were school photos of her and her brother, snapshots of holidays with the tent trailer, a few photos from Australia, and several wedding pictures. In the largest frame was a family portrait showing Grandpa and Grandma, uncles and aunts, cousins, and even the youngest uncle's dogs. Everyone was looking straight into the lens, as the photographer had tried to get a good shot of all the faces on the memorable day when they celebrated Grandpa and Grandma's 40th wedding anniversary. It had taken a lot of shoving and pulling before everyone was in place. Unfortunately, the photographer – whom he had personally hired, by the way – had not managed to make everyone smile at the camera at the right moment.

When the girl came home on weekends and hung her coat on the coat rack, she would always see that picture out of the corner of her eye and try to ignore it.

But today, she immediately saw that the picture was damaged. The glass in the frame was broken, and someone had tried to remove the shards from the frame. A few bits still glistened in the corners. The bare photo was still in the frame and was almost undamaged. Only her mother's face in the photo had been severely scratched by the breaking glass. His face, just next to hers, was unscathed. It was the only smiling face in the picture.

8 May, 1992 – First wedding anniversary

For the first time, I felt happy. In my mind, I would occasionally list all the things to celebrate: I had a nice job, a nice apartment, friendly neighbors, some good friends I was always welcome with, a surrogate child who adored me, the relationship with my mother was still improving, and Bram and Annet I could always unconditionally go to.

I regularly drove to Bilthoven in my second-hand car. It was a dark red Citroën BX, and I glided stately along the road in it.

That Friday, I picked up my mother in Leusden, where she had moved after the divorce. She was still working part-time, but thoroughly enjoying her newfound freedom. With the proceeds of the remaining twelve Krugerrands, which supplemented her modest income, for the first time in her life she no longer had money worries. She had gratefully accepted the coins without asking a single question. Of course, without explanation, she also understood where they came from. She relaxed, and by the day became a nicer person.

From time to time, she also went with me to Edgar and Greetje's, who always received her warmly and where Junior darted around her as if she were his grandmother. And she was only too happy to let that happen, since neither I nor Bram seemed to be going to deliver her any grandchildren of her own.

Enthusiastically, she hugged me once she got into the car. 'Gee, I'm looking forward to tonight, are you?'

'Sure, have you thought of the card?'

We were treating Bram and Annet to a weekend getaway in a wellness resort with all the trimmings to celebrate their first wedding anniversary. I had made the reservation and paid the money for the hotel. My mother had bought a voucher for a five-course dinner and written a nice card. On my lap, I put my name under her scribble.

With a satisfied sigh, my mother put the card in her bag and said, 'Let's go.'

The cheese fondue that we now traditionally ate at Bram and Annet's place was delicious again, and it was a relaxed and pleasant evening all together. Of course, Bram and Annet didn't need the gift at all. But it was clear from their delighted looks that they were very happy with it.

December 25, 1985 – Weekend getaway

They never went on a weekend away. He thought it was too expensive, and although Mum had fancied a weekend away, she would have preferred to go with a friend instead. So, she didn't insist.

For Christmas, the company he was still working for at the time splashed out. All employees and their spouses were invited on a weekend trip to a five-star hotel on the coast, where they would be treated to a sumptuous Christmas dinner. Down in the basement of the hotel, there was a large swimming pool with a sauna next to it. He couldn't pass that up, and he thought Mum should come along.

She objected that it would mean having to miss their daughter's birthday and that she did not fancy his colleagues, whom he despised anyway, but he was implacable. So, on Christmas Day, they put on their best clothes and drove in silence to the hotel. Arriving there, it turned out to be a madhouse, as the others had already arrived for drinks hours before. The invitation to join them had never reached him, so they stood uneasily and soberly among the other guests, who were already tipsy, or even quite drunk.

The booze had made everyone a bit less formal than usual. Colleague after colleague came to meet Mum, and she was kissed warmly by all the men. They didn't understand how the strange fellow had such a nice wife.

The company director, in particular, who would have preferred him to leave the company tomorrow, did not hesitate. 'De Wit, what a beautiful wife you have. Can I dance with her?' And before he could say no, Mum was pulled onto the dance floor.

She spent the whole evening dancing with all his colleagues. It was a dinner dance, so there wasn't much sitting down either.

He became increasingly angry, especially because she wouldn't dance with him. He couldn't dance very well, but she could. More and more cheerfully, she danced with one colleague after another, while he sipped the free drinks at the bar in disgust.

His colleagues on the dance floor undressed Mum with their eyes. The idea of what might happen at the pool or sauna next day bothered him. He decided that they would go home that same evening. And instead of waiting any longer, he would announce immediately after New Year that he was quitting his job.

9 May, 1992 – Waiting list

Saturday morning, I was at Edgar and Greetje's house. There was trampling and cheering in the hallway, then, 'Aunt Kiki, Aunt Kiki is here!' The door opened and Junior flew around my neck. He half strangled me and planted his wet lips on my cheeks. 'Have you come to see my new train?'

Together with Edgar, we watched the toy train for a while. We were not allowed to touch it, of course; Junior wanted to drive it all by himself.

'Yes, you are very good at that, son,' said Edgar. 'Aunt Kiki has something to discuss some things with us. If you play with the train some more, then we'll sit down at the table.'

With coffee in front of us, we looked at all the densely printed sheets of paper which Edgar had already laid out. In the office, he had collected information of all primary schools in Amsterdam via the Internet. Junior had to be registered at the right school as soon as possible, because there were long waiting lists everywhere. And these were not only for primary schools, but also for a number of – usually the best – secondary schools.

Through a colleague with older children, Edgar had learned that the coveted spot in the secondary school of first choice, was only attainable with good reports and the right primary school. It was strange, though, that by the time a child was five his entire school career had to be carefully mapped out.

Greetje wanted Junior to go to Reformed Lyceum South later. We had to take that into account when choosing a primary school. So, it had to be a protestant school. She had also always been to schools 'with the Bible', as they were called, and she wasn't any the worse for it, she said.

The idea horrified me.

4 January, 1986 – School reunion

Mum, as usual, was the first to wake up, so she immediately heard the phone at ten o'clock in the morning. It was a classmate from her daughter's grammar school. Mum called the girl out of bed and kept looking questioningly at her as she answered the phone.

The classmate told her that a class reunion would be organized in a week's time. And it would be nice if the girl would come, because then the whole class would be there.

Her entire secondary school period had passed by the girl at lightning speed, spending six years without friends, the only unbeliever among the Pharisees. Six years in which they had made frantic attempts to convert her, and when that failed, had ignored her. Years in which there had only been a focus on academic achievement, no room for learning any social skills, and in which many teachers even considered mutual bullying quite normal.

Her biology teacher had once helped a girl who had unexpectedly become pregnant by a classmate, through to her final exams. She had to work from home, as she had no longer been welcome at school with her fat belly. Personally, the girl had always found what that teacher did a brilliant example of Christian charity. But the other teachers had apparently seen it differently; the biology teacher had been ignored by them as much as possible since then. And the child's father, of course, was not stopped from finishing school. At school, not at home like the girl.

'Hello, are you still there?' she heard her classmate's voice ask.

She ignored it and put the receiver down.

20 May, 1993 – A real auntie now

Today Junior got to 'try' again for a day at primary school. Greetje had sprained her ankle and Edgar couldn't get time off. Secretly, I was pleased. Now I got to take Junior to school.

Hand-in-hand, we walked the few blocks toward what Junior called 'the big school'. From the beginning of the street, you could already hear the children in the schoolyard. Junior let go of my hand and started skipping ahead. 'Wait with crossing, please,' I called out.

At the gate, we were met by Miss Janice. 'Hey, Edgar, are you having a nice day with us today? We're going to have fun. Today we are going to read and write.'

'Well, I can already write my name,' Junior said.

'Really, how clever.'

The teacher looked at me questioningly. 'I don't think we've met. I was expecting one of his parents.'

As I explained why they had not been able to come, Junior happily crowed, 'This is my Auntie Kiki, she took me to school.'

'Well, that's clear then,' Janice said. 'Say goodbye to your aunt, and we'll go in.'

'Bye bye, see you later, Auntie Kiki,' Junior said, and then he walked with the teacher. Just before the school entrance, he turned around once more and waved at me.

9 January, 1986 – Goodbye

Early in the morning, a small coach turned onto the square in front of Amstel train station. The group of economics students had been eagerly awaiting it for half an hour. Today, they would leave for a study trip to Frankfurt, where they would be visiting a large investment bank. They had organized it all themselves, and now they were proudly waiting for the coach to pick them up.

They had agreed with their professor how many credits they could earn if they jointly submitted a report of the trip to her. They had shared the costs of the coach, and to reduce the other costs they would spend the night in a youth hostel, and also cook and eat there.

As they were cramming their bags into the luggage compartment, a car suddenly drove into the square, honking loudly.

The girl recognized her Uncle Hans' big red car, and he immediately got out on one side. Her mother got out on the other side, and they walked towards the group of students.

'We've come to see you off,' the uncle said.

'Can someone please help carry this?' Mum asked.

From the boot came two large boxes filled with cans of soft drinks, crisps, a large bag of Dutch licorice, and biscuits with pink icing on top, all of which were happily carried onto the bus.

Mum kissed the girl and wished her a good journey. The uncle pressed some German Marks into her hand. 'You treat everyone to a nice drink tonight, dear. Have fun.'

The boys shook hands with him enthusiastically and everyone kissed Mum. When the bus left, they sat backwards on the benches to wave back, as if it were an old school trip.

'Gosh, what cool parents you have,' one of her fellow students said to the girl.

6 June, 1993 – End of the ride

I toured the ring road. Just like that, without no particular purpose. It was a lovely day, and I had just wanted to go for a drive. The windows were slightly open, Queen was blaring from the loudspeaker, and I was singing along loudly and out of tune at the top of my voice. I decided that I would drive to my mother's place to watch a really bad girl movie with her on the sofa, and giggle together in front of the TV with a glass of white wine in hand. Yes, yummy!

Too bad, a traffic jam was ahead. I had to join the back of the queue. I turned off the radio, because the other cars were now quite close, and it was a bit embarrassing that they could hear me sing.

The men around me were judging my Citroën BX. Yes indeed, all mine. With that lovely hydraulic suspension. Proudly, I sat upright behind the wheel. But after an initial inspection, they didn't give my car a second look. I myself was looked at all the better.

In the car next to me were two young boys. Leaning back, with baseball caps on, they watched me with horny glances, safely from behind the windows. I tried to ignore them as we slowly crept across the tarmac.

In the distance I saw flashing lights and a police car askew on the verge. An accident? For a moment I had to think back to that night more than five years ago now. Yikes. But I didn't see an ambulance, so it shouldn't be too bad.

Strange, all those cops on the street. When I got even closer, I saw that the police officers allowed most cars to pass through after a minor delay, but a few unlucky ones were pointed to the right. And these were diverted down the motorway in a small procession, a motorbike cop in front and also one behind. Golly, it seemed like they only picked out the second-hand cars.

Now it was my turn. Open your window! gestured the officer, annoyed.

'Good afternoon, ma'am. Today we're doing a major traffic check, ma'am. We'll check your papers, the condition of your car, and whether you have any outstanding fines, for example, ma'am. If you could join those cars there in the emergency lane, the motorbike officers will escort you to the car park where we'll safely do all the checks, ma'am.'

The many repetitions of the word 'ma'am' got on my nerves. How could I get out of this?

'Um, but I'm in a bit of a hurry. Why are you picking me out now?' I asked.

'We pick people at random, ma'am. Where do you need to go in such a hurry then?'

I didn't answer that.

'We assume your cooperation, mind you. Most people don't object. And there is no need at all if you have nothing to hide.' Remarkably, he suddenly had stopped saying 'ma'am' at the end of every sentence. And he didn't look bored now, like before. He gave me a piercing look.

'No, sorry, but I'm just in a bit of a hurry. So, I line up there?' I pointed to the rear car in the emergency lane.

'Indeed,' the cop said, handing me back my papers.

As I drove away, I saw in my rear-view mirror that the cop stood on the road wide-legged, watching me go, saying something into his walkie-talkie. Oh dear. The baseball caps had to come along, too, and joined the queue behind me. They were suddenly much less chatty.

After a short ride between two motorbike cops, we reached a car park where we were met by a large group of cops, several police cars, and a large police van. Each car was directed into its own trap between orange cones and surrounded by a bunch of cops, like flies on a fresh turd.

Again, the circus act with the papers. But now I had to get out of the car.

One of the officers ordered me to blow into the nozzle of an alcohol tester. 'Keep blowing steadily until I tell you to stop.' While I was blowing, the other officers inspected the technical condition of my car. It would make you nervous anyway.

I heard a dry click and the officer said, 'You can stop now. Just a moment. Yes, fine, you haven't been drinking. Would you just follow my colleague to that big police van?'

Meekly, accompanied by another cop, I walked across the car park. Next to me, the baseball caps were just driving away.

The passenger turned down the window and yelled: 'Hey, Grandma, pay your parking fines properly, huh?' Then they dashed off, howling and full throttle. The cop next to me thought it was pretty funny.

On the bus, I was taken to a small room. There were two hard benches, with a tiny table between them, screwed to the wall. 'Please sit down, one of my colleagues will join you in a moment.'

I had little choice. I folded myself onto one of the benches and waited for the next officer. He came walking in after a few minutes, adjusting his uniform jacket. He greeted me, but kept his gaze tightly focused on my papers, which he held in his hand. He looked vaguely familiar, but I couldn't quite place him.

'Ms De Wit. So you were in a hurry, I understand.' It sounded like a question.

'Hmmmm, yes,' I said vaguely. Where did I know this guy from, anyway?

'My name is De Jong, Constable Geert de Jong. Look, if you give me all the information I need, I can take a quick look to see if everything is OK and it won't take long. All right?' He was looking at me full on now.

I just nodded. Officer Geert, from Wibautstraat police station. I saw that he had also recognized me.

25 January, 1986 – Birthday party

Today Mum turned fifty. Time for a party, everyone thought. For weeks, they had been quietly making traditional Sarah dolls. Early in the morning, a hideous one had been put on the doorstep in front of the house for everyone to see she was now an old woman.

But there was no big party. For weeks, they had walked to the mailbox every day to fish out the invitation card. And when it took an awfully long time for it to arrive, they had called each other to find out if others had already received an invitation. But they had not.

Cautiously, the youngest uncle had finally asked Mum exactly where and when the party would be.

'There will be no party, because there's nothing to celebrate,' she had snapped at him.

Deeply shocked, he had drifted off. It couldn't be true, could it? No dancing in line and no free drinks? Surely, the family had been denied a nice evening of celebration?

He didn't like the way she had said this to everyone. So, today he had no present for her. There was nothing to celebrate; she had said it herself.

'If you go on like this, you better watch it,' she told him carelessly. 'I'll leave you.'

'Do so at your own peril,' he said, 'then you'll find out how that turns out for you.'

8 May, 1996 – Departure

This Wednesday started festively, with coffee and cake which I brought for my colleagues, to celebrate the fact that I was finally leaving for a holiday. Other than a few casual days off, I had never taken holidays before. And now I was going to Australia. It was too good to be true, and everyone was eagerly biting into pieces of cake, while they looked at the pictures in my now well-thumbed travel guide. I had brought it with me to show them where I was going.

Freek and Jolanda had a present for me – a sleeping mask for the plane. There was a hologram in it which, when you moved your head slightly, made it look as if your – large – eyes opened and closed in time. Edgar and Greetje had given me an overpriced outdoor cap with a big sun visor the night before. My mother had handed me an envelope with three hundred-guilder notes ('For you, dear. Bram gets the same from me. Do something nice with that, please.') And Junior had bought me a big bag of mints with his pocket money ('For on the plane, Auntie Kiki, so your ears don't pop during take-off and landing.') Edgar stood beaming at me from behind his plate of cake.

When the phone rang on my desk, we ignored it; clients could wait. But after half an hour it kept ringing almost continuously.

'Just wait,' Edgar said. 'I'll switch it over to reception,' and he picked up the handset to do so. But apparently he had someone on the line right away, because his finger lingered over the buttons and he pressed the handset to his ear, listening with intense concentration.

Visibly startled, he turned his eyes to me and put the phone back on the hook.

He looked straight at me, and I saw immediately that he had no good news. With weak knees, I sat down on my desk chair.

'What is it?' I asked him.

Edgar cleared his throat. 'Sorry, guys, something nasty has come up. We must continue this party another time.' All the while, he kept staring at me.

The murmur of the other colleagues immediately hushed. 'Yes, take your cake to your own desks, see you later,' Edgar said.

Uncertainly, they looked from him to me, but soon they had all left my office. And I just sat there, waiting for what was to come.

'That was your Uncle Hans. Your mother is not well.'

Every word echoed loudly in my head: YOUR... MOTHER... IS... NOT... WELL!!!

Before I knew it, I was standing with Bram, Annet, Hans, and Tom in a cramped little room on one of the top floors of the Diakonessenhuis hospital in Utrecht, at my mother's ICU bed. Edgar, who had brought me here in his car, sat somewhere nervously down the corridor.

With horror, I looked at the beeping machines and the many tubes and cords connected to my mother somewhere under the sheets. My proud mother, who lay here like a shrunken mummy, gray, with hollowed cheeks, uncombed hair, and no make-up. Carefully I felt for her hand.

'I want to get out of here,' she whispered, giving a squeeze to my fingers.

'What happened?' I asked. She didn't answer but looked at Uncle Hans.

He answered for her. 'Your mother had quite a stomach ache three years ago, and we took her to the doctor. She felt something in her abdomen. They wanted to operate immediately, because they suspected she had an aneurysm even then. But your mother refused, didn't you, Judith?'

'Yes,' she said.

'Mum, why?' cried Bram. 'And why didn't you tell us anything?' he asked Uncle Hans accusingly, without waiting for Mum's answer.

'Calm down, son. Your mother made an informed decision. The operation was risky, and she wanted to enjoy her freedom for a few more years. It was more likely to happen without surgery than with it. And she didn't want to burden you with it. I had to swear not to tell you.

'I wish I could have done more for you,' she said in one last, lucid moment.

'Sshh, hush,' I said awkwardly, horrified, and I held her hand, which already felt cold. My mother's frightened eyes shot back and forth between Bram and me. 'Please don't be angry. I only wanted the best for you.'

That was the last thing she said.

Suddenly all the alarms on the devices went off, and almost immediately people in white coats dashed into the room. My mother seemed unconscious and hung limply in the pillows.

'Everyone out, wait in the family room at the end of the corridor,' one of them commanded us.

We waited there in tense silence for what was to come. Annet took care of Bram, and Tom took care of Hans. I called Edgar in because I needed someone to cling to, and he was part of the family after all.

After an eternity, there was a knock on the door and a young woman in a white coat entered. Wearily, she pushed some hair out of her face and sat down with us.

'You are related to Mrs. Judith de Bruin?' she asked. When we confirmed with nods, she introduced herself as Doctor Verhoeven. She told us that she had seen my mother in early 1994 with a pulsating tumor, obviously an aneurysm of the aorta. Despite her insistence, my mother had refused surgery. And as a doctor, she had to respect her choice, even though she thought it was an unwise one.

So, this morning, the aneurysm had started leaking. On the abdominal ultrasound just now, it was visible that there was now considerable bleeding; the aneurysm had ruptured.

There was a moment of silence as we tried to process that.

'And now?' asked Bram. 'Is there still time to do that operation today or tomorrow, after all?'

'I wish there was, but unfortunately, that is not an option. Your mother has already lost a lot of blood by now. Moreover, her overall condition is not so good. Diabetes causes her blood sugar to fluctuate too much, and her kidney function has not been good for years. An operation now won't work, and she probably wouldn't even survive the anesthesia. I am sorry.'

'But wait a minute, does this mean she is going to die?' I asked in a strained voice.

'That is indeed what I am trying to make clear.'

Stiffened with horror, we dared not to ask anything more, afraid of answers we didn't want to hear.

But we didn't have to ask. The doctor told us that she would now go back to my mother to check that everything had been done to make her as comfortable and pain-free as possible with sedatives, morphine, and oxygen. She promised us that she would return as soon as possible to allow us to be with our mother and say goodbye.

And we did. We sat with her for a while longer. At first, she was still alive, her chest moving up and down laboriously. But after a few minutes, she was suddenly dead. Just like that, boom, from one moment to the next she was no more.

The Australia trip could not take place. Instead, we buried my mother. Annet and I combed her hair, painted her lips and her nails. Bram screwed the coffin shut himself, and carried it to the grave together with Hans, Tom, and Edgar. At the grave (the most beautiful spot in the cemetery, for which we had paid extra without complaining), touching words were spoken, Junior read a poem, and we drank Prosecco with everyone present. Then there was a sumptuous five-course meal at a fine restaurant, with wine flowing profusely. No one was talking about the planned holiday anymore.

1 February, 1986 – Gone too far

That Saturday morning, the girl had only gotten out of bed late after waking up to a piercing silence in the house. Mum was probably out shopping, as she always prepared a lot of food when she came home on weekends. But where was he?

As gently as she could, she opened the doors of all the bedrooms. There was no one there. Barefoot, she snuck down the stairs. No, no one in the living room either. She walked to the kitchen to make a cup of tea and wait for Mum to return with the groceries.

Just behind the door, he sat on a chair at the kitchen table in front of his plate with half a slice of buttered bread. Shit.

He didn't move. It seemed like he wasn't breathing. The knife in his hand, with which he had buttered his sandwich, pointed with the tip upwards. She followed his gaze and saw that it was fixed on Mum, who came walking up the garden path with a big bag of groceries.

Slowly and silently, he rose from his chair, the knife still in his hand.

The struggle was already over when Mum stepped through the kitchen door. He walked out of the kitchen without a word, and Mum took care of her daughter, who decided then and there that she would go to the police one more time.

2 All actions have consequences

13 December, 2004 – Helping the police

The police officer is extremely friendly and her colleague in the corner is probably a great guy too, but I still feel totally uncomfortable. And I leave the cup of coffee they gave me untouched. This cup of coffee reminds me too much of another conversation with the police a long time ago.

It seems clear to me what they want from me. The whole story, all the facts, and preferably a confession, too, at once.

The letter I received from them scared the hell out of me. Under the bold heading ('Invitation to a police interview') it said in officialese that I was invited to help them with their enquiries into the death on 4 March, 1988 of Mr. Robert de Wit.

And it also said somewhere that a number of Krugerrands had been stolen from him. By me, or so they seem to think. I have not been able to remember the rest of the letter, although I have read it at least a dozen times.

After the initial shock, I had phoned the offices of Buergher & De Wyth in De Bilt, where Annet still works. They had assured me that they would pass on my message to her, and that Master Van Rijn would contact me as soon as possible. Fortunately, she did so quickly, and I was able to drop by the office immediately.

First, she had concentrated on reading the letter of invitation.

'Now there's a strange story, indeed,' she concluded when she had finished reading. 'Surely, they will first have to prove that the man died of a crime, and then also that you committed this crime. Tssssss... And that bit about a theft also seems rather difficult for them to prove. You could easily have bought some Krugerrands yourself. Look, Bram told me that you took those things from his house, but taking something from your own inheritance is not quite the same as theft. I'd have to look into that, but it all seems rather far-fetched to me.'

The question which had been burning on my lips for a while had blurted out: 'Why don't they just arrest me? Now I get an invitation like I'm going to a party.'

'Good question. You know, if they had already built a solid case against you and had a lot of evidence, they would definitely have picked you up. The fact that you are now invited to help them with their enquiries, is actually a good thing. They are probably not so sure of what happened and have not got their facts straight. They might want to do a little fishing to see what they catch, and whether they've got a case.'

'But why now, after all these years?'

'Well, they must be in a hurry. The statute of limitations for murder is 18 years. So, they don't have that much longer. And apparently, something akin to suspicion has been simmering in the background since 1988. Or maybe someone made an incriminating statement. Someone who thinks they saw something, maybe. No idea. But it's now or never for them. In principle, you don't even have to go; or you can just ignore the invitation. I'm just afraid they won't give up so easily, and they may even put you in police custody if you don't show up.

'Thursday is actually inconvenient for me, but I can reschedule some of my appointments and then I'll just go with you as your defense lawyer. OK?' she had asked.

So now we are sitting here together. Luckily, the police officers had put on sour faces but otherwise had not made a fuss when I introduced Master Annet as my lawyer.

They've just told me I don't have to answer their questions, and Annet and I have agreed that she will cough vigorously if I have to keep my mouth shut. As long as she doesn't, I just have to answer all questions, preferably as briefly and concisely as possible.

The questions start innocently enough. What my name is, my date and place of birth, where I live. What my parents' names, dates of birth and death are, whether I have siblings, and so on.

Then they want to know all sorts of things that still seem innocent. From what car I drive, to how much I earn, how I got my beautiful apartment on Stadhouderskade, and a whole host of other questions. On the clock on the wall, I see that more than an hour has already passed.

Annet coughs and intervenes. She wants to know why the officers are asking me all these questions. Are they relevant? Her client does not understand why she has been invited for an interview about the 1988 accident from the consequences of which the driver, her father, sadly died. And this despite her client's heroic efforts to stem the arterial bleeding from his neck, right there at the scene of the accident, while she herself was also injured. And how about theft? What a bunch of nonsense it all is.

I am greatly relieved that Annet seems to have stopped the flow of questions. For a moment, I can catch my breath.

But the cops are not smiling kindly now. After some skirmishes back and forth between the officers and Annet, we agree that I will make a short statement. I do so, exactly as I agreed with Annet two days ago. It contains whatever I stated in 1988 and closes with the firm statement that I have not stolen anything, absolutely nothing. When it is finally all in writing and Annet has ironed out the last mistakes, I sign it.

'As far as we're concerned, that's the end of it,' Annet says as we are get up to leave. 'I assume that, within a reasonable time, my client will hear that she is no longer a suspect of any crime. And if I may say, on a personal note: this is all ridiculous! Never, as a lawyer, have I experienced anything like it.'

20 December, 2004 – Arrested

I just had a nice cup of coffee from the coffee machine I treated myself to. And now I'm sitting in front of the newspaper, which I have placed open in front of me on the dining table. The doorbell rings, and on the video doorbell screen I can see two uniformed police officers standing in front of my door. Geez, what now? Stunned, I hear them ask if they can come in. After a brief hesitation, I press the button to open the door for them. I shouldn't have, because they arrest me (they are 'taking me into custody,' they say), and within two minutes I'm in the back of their police car heading for the nearest police station. Thank God they didn't handcuff me. Once at the station, they take my fingerprints and nick my passport, which I had to bring with me.

What happens next fixes itself as disjointed fragments in my memory: my arraignment before the examining magistrate, who speaks a few stern words (I have no idea what exactly); several interrogations with the same questions over and over again; the smelly police holding cell with the stainless-steel loo and the hard wooden bench; my repeated protests and demands for my lawyer. It is a confusing and shocking experience.

At night, in the police cell, I pick aimlessly at a piece of loose plaster until my nails, still black from the fingerprint ink, bleed one by one. The piece of plaster finally falls to the ground... and dozens more pieces follow before dawn.

It is not until the next day that I am allowed to speak to Annet, and finally I am even allowed to go home. But my passport remains with the police. I'm still a suspect, so I am not allowed to just go on a trip. I am so shocked by what has happened that, once I get home, I go straight to bed and only get out on Christmas Day (my birthday) when there is a long press on the doorbell.

It's Annet and Bram who, without further ado, put me in the shower, let me put on clean clothes and eat a plate of Brinta-porridge. Then Greetje and Edgar arrive. Edgar junior also has a birthday today, but will not be able to attend. He is now a tall, lanky young man of almost two meters, who graduated from HAVO secondary school last summer and is now in Australia, eagerly taking advantage of exchange program opportunities.

Depressed, we still try to create something of a Christmas atmosphere. We do our best with the wine and the snacks that Greetje has brought, and together we crawl behind my laptop late in the evening to Skype with Junior.

On the face of it, no one understands why I was arrested, although I see Annet and Bram exchanging the occasional meaningful glance.

'If it gets too hot under your feet there, Auntie, you'll come to Australia, won't you?' says Junior, grinning at me from the screen of my laptop.

10 January, 2005 – Summoned

On Monday morning, just before I am about to leave for work, the doorbell rings. I'm immediately wary and first check through the video doorbell to see if it's another cop. But the man on the pavement is not wearing a uniform, so I dare to open the door.

'Ms De Wit?' the man asks.

Oh no, I should have left the door closed after all.

'Kiki de Wit?' he insists.

I don't say anything, but he pushes a large A4-sized envelope into my hands. He also immediately holds a form under my nose and wants to give me a pen, which I can use to sign for receipt.

Well, I have no intention of doing that. I slam the door shut in the middle of his surprised face and run up the stairs to my flat, tear open the envelope, and start reading the letter with the blue logo:

Summons to appear in court

Sector no.:	10	
File no.:	15/10-00157-2	
Sequence no.:	0001	
To:	Name:	De Wit
	First Name(s):	Kiki
	Date of birth:	25 December, 1965
	Place of birth:	Port Augusta (Australia)
	Address:	288 III Stadhouderskade, Amsterdam

I hereby summon you to appear, on 3 March, 2005 at 2:30pm before the Amsterdam Criminal Court, 220 Parnassusweg, in order to stand trial as a defendant on the following charges:

1. *That you on 4 March, 1988 on the A9 Motorway, off Pampusweg near exit number 3, did unlawfully kill your father, Mr. Robert de Wit, born 2 April, 1941 in...*

'Shit!' I think again... and then nothing for quite a while. It's as if a short circuit has occurred in my head and things must be rebooted. In the meantime, my brain is not working.

I try to read what it says again and see a whole bunch of numbers from the Dutch Penal Code. They must have to do with murder. And then something about a lawyer and several witnesses who apparently told all sorts of things about me. In the list of witnesses, I see some unknown names, but I also see three acquaintances: Fenna, Wieger, and Officer Geert. *'What the fuck?'*

Now everything will come out and I will go to prison. I am freezing cold just at the very idea.

Shivering, I sit on my sofa until suddenly the phone rings. It's my secretary at work, clearly relieved to hear my voice. When am I coming in, and am I all right? Truthfully, I tell her I'm sitting on the couch with a pounding headache and forgot to call in sick.

'It doesn't matter, dear,' she says motherly, 'I'll do that for you straight away.' She wishes me a speedy recovery and hangs up.

I immediately spring into action. I call Annet and tell her I have received a summons. She has not yet received anything herself, even though it should be known that she is my lawyer. It all seems unreal.

22 March, 2005 – First day of session

So, it IS unreal, like I'm not actually there, but watching an absurdist courtroom drama with an unlikely script on television. The prosecutor just told me why I'm here as a defendant. I allegedly killed my father out of jealousy or misplaced vindictiveness. And what's more, I allegedly took the opportunity to steal some valuables from my father. My motive for all this, he argues, is that I wanted revenge, as will be evident from the statements of witnesses he will call during the trial. He has demanded a custodial sentence of at least six years. It made me cringe.

One of the judges – the woman in the middle – asked if I had understood everything, and she has asked me how I want to plead: guilty or not guilty.

After glancing at Annet, I say, 'Madam, I heard what he said, but I don't understand it. I really have no idea why I'm sitting here and no, of course I'm *not* guilty. This must all be a big mistake.' As Annet implored me, I say this in a calm tone, articulating clearly and looking straight at the judge. I would believe it myself.

'Good, then I ask the prosecutor to call his first witness now.'

An elderly lady is brought in by the usher. She is visibly nervous as she takes the oath and avoids looking in my direction. I really have no idea who she is, and her name (Mrs. Groenteman) means nothing to me either.

Once the woman has taken the oath, the prosecutor begins: 'Mrs. Groenteman, can you tell us where you were on 4 March, 1988 around five in the afternoon?'

'Yes, sir. I was in the car with my husband, and we were driving on the A9 motorway. We were almost at the

Diemen exit. That's where we were going to babysit our grandchildren that night.'

'Tell us in your own words what you heard and saw there, please.'

'The weather was bad and it started to snow, so my husband drove carefully. He always did. In the distance, we saw a car suddenly making a strange lurch, as if someone had given a tug on the steering wheel. Well, that car first almost ended up on the verge, and then it shot diagonally across the road to the left. There, it crashed into the barrier. I had never heard such a bang; it was deafening. My husband was terribly frightened, too.'

'And then what happened?'

'It happened very quickly. My husband put our car on the hard shoulder, and I ran between traffic to the car.' Now she takes a quick glance in my direction, but immediately looks away again. 'Yes, and then, um, so I saw it.'

'Go ahead, tell us what you saw.'

'Well, I saw that the girl was on top of that man, restraining him. He looked terrified.'

'What exactly do you mean when you say she was restraining him?'

'Well, he was laying there against the left door, and she was hovering over him with her hand on his mouth. Blood was gushing from his neck. I could not believe it. It happened very quickly. Suddenly the man went limp. And then I was pushed aside by my husband. He stayed with the car, and then I called the police and an ambulance via the talking post.'

'And you're sure her hand was on his mouth?'

'Yes, she only removed it when my husband started pulling on the car door. And then she suddenly pressed that hand on his neck.'

'Only then? So, after she had pressed his mouth shut for a while, and only when your husband started pulling on the car door?'

'Yes.'

One of the judges puts in, 'So you are sure, ma'am, it was after your husband opened the door of the car?'

'Yes,' the woman whispers.

Then it's Anne's turn. She asks the woman why she waited so long to make this statement. After all, it's been a long time since the accident happened. And besides, this all contradicts what her husband told the police at the time. He stated that I had briskly tried to save my father by pressing my hand on the wound in his neck.

She and her husband have always argued about what exactly happened, the woman says. And the police at the time only took her husband's statement and did not ask her anything. She purses her lips and says that since her husband's death two years ago, she has found much comfort at the local church. Her faith has deepened, and it commands her to speak the truth. She quotes from the Bible, 3 John 1:4:

> *I have no greater joy than to hear that*
> *my children are walking in the truth.*

With her head held high, she leaves the room. It is completely silent.

Then it is the turn of the second witness. And there she walks into court, nicely coiffed and manicured, on high heels. Older, but well-preserved and, by the looks of it, still an obnoxious bitch. Swinging her hips, she walks towards the stand, pointed out to her by the usher. She doesn't give me a glance.

Only after Mrs. Fenna Annika Burger-de Boer is sworn in does she stealthily glance in my direction for a moment. She is obviously enjoying her leading role in this drama. And she's about to take her revenge on me, you can see that. For what exactly, we will of course soon find out.

De Boer, a quite common name and I'm sure there are lots of people called that, but it must be that she married Wieger. Together, they make a nice couple, I'm sure. I whisper in Annet's ear what I'm thinking, and she nods, writes something on her notepad on the table in front of her, and observes Fenna closely.

Fenna answers all questions put to her by the prosecutor. The following story emerges: The victim (she says 'the defendant's father' and looks viciously aside) – her boyfriend at the time – had asked her to marry him when she became pregnant. Since he had just divorced and suspected that I (again 'the defendant') would not like it very much if he married a much younger woman, they decided to break the news to me together. Therefore, her lover had gone to pick up 'the defendant' by car. On the motorway, things must have gone wrong, and he was badly injured by something I must have done; there is really no other way. He later died of his injuries in hospital, so it's my fault he's dead. And I must have also stolen a number of valuables from his house after his death. Because while she and her baby ('the defendant's half-sister') were barely making ends meet, six months later I gave her four Krugerrands that I had supposedly found in his house. And to her knowledge, there should have been more than just four, so I must have pocketed the rest. She had earlier submitted two pledge slips from the Haarlemmerdijk pawn shop to the court as evidence. No, she has no actual evidence that I physically hurt Robert, but she just knows

I did. He also used to say that he considered 'the defendant' capable of anything.

Precisely because she had heard nothing about Robert's death at the time, her suspicions were aroused. Sure enough, it also says in Robert's death certificate that he died an unnatural death. And so 'the defendant' had a motive for murder. 'Well then!' she concludes triumphantly.

'How does she know what's in that death certificate?' I think.

'Whether there is a motive here, we leave that for the court to judge,' says Annet, taking the floor. 'And Krugerrands are freely available. How were they stolen? Is there any evidence of that? My client has stated that she got those things from her father, and she was free to give them away. And what does she get in return? Nothing but incriminations!'

The judges nod affably. The middle judge tersely casts an angry glance at the prosecutor, but I don't see that.

'Mr. De Wit died as a result of a car accident. This is indeed an unnatural death, but such things happen. Why would my client steal from your loved one? By the way, do you know that my client has rejected her father's inheritance?' asks Annet in conclusion.

It is obvious from her surprised look and gaping mouth that this is a surprise for Fenna. The prosecutor fiddles uneasily with his robe.

Fenna is thanked for her presence, and she trips to the exit, where Wieger is waiting for her.

Slightly irritated, the female judge asks the prosecutor if he wants to call any more witnesses. Cheerfully, he says he does indeed. He calls for Police Constable Geert de Jong, who testifies that in 1986, at Wibautstraat police station, I tried to make a false report of rape by the victim.

And I had definitely appeared homicidal. He thought even then that my father would be better off staying away from the defendant.

One of the male judges cuts that short. He looks at Geert warningly and instructs him to stick to the facts.

'Boy, what a story', says Annet, when given the floor. She also has some questions for this witness: whether he has something concrete to say, has evidence for the alleged murder or the alleged theft? No, he doesn't.

And whether she can see the 1986 police report, because it was not in the court file? No, she cannot, because no report was filed, according to Geert.

'Why not?' asks Annet, seemingly innocently.

The story which I had come to the police station with then was clearly not true, according to Geert. And to prevent me from making a false report, for which I could then also be prosecuted, he had personally ensured that nothing was recorded. And nothing had been filed either. So, in effect, he had done me a favor.

'But then how are you so sure that my client here is the same person who appeared at the Wibautstraat police station on 2 February, 1986?' asks Annette. 'If there is no report, and nothing was put on file, then surely there are no records, such as name, place of residence, and so on?'

'No, that is right. But on 6 June, 1993, I encountered the accused at a traffic control. I recognized her immediately. She stood out because she was behaving suspiciously.'

'Whoa, wait a minute. Why was she acting suspiciously?'

'She immediately wanted to leave right away, evading the traffic control. Usually, people then have something to hide.'

'And did she?'

'Um, well, she had a broken rear light. She was fined for that, too.'

'Aha, and so that's how you got hold of my client's personal data,' Annet observes.

The prosecutor interrupts, 'Does the defendant deny that she is the same person who appeared on 2 February, 1986 at the Wibautstraat police station in Amsterdam to report a crime?'

Ideally, I would deny that, but Annet advised me against it. So, I therefore answer with a simple, 'No, I don't deny that.'

Annet immediately goes on with questions about the constable's career, whether he hasn't been able to get promoted after all those long years with the police. From police officer at a desk job to constable with the traffic police is not exactly a dream career.

Geert seems startled by that question, says that he is having a great time with traffic police and has never had any other ambitions.

'Oh,' asks Annet, 'so the fact that during your time at Wibautstraat police station you did not want to take any statement, not even a single report of rape or assault, that has nothing to do with the fact that you were disciplined and thus sidetracked?'

The judges are visibly surprised.

'Say, you listen to me carefully,' says Geert, pointing his finger at Annet. 'I—'

'We'll have none of that,' says the female judge. 'Just answer the defendant lawyer's questions! I remind you that you are under oath, and we can quite easily check whether you have ever recorded a rape report. And for that matter, whether you have ever been disciplined, and if so, for what.'

The prosecutor turns white and Geert seems to explode. 'Pffff, what nonsense this all is.' He crosses his arms in front of his chest and looks sullenly ahead. He then refuses to answer any other questions.

Annet says decisively that she has no further questions for this witness anyway and looks intently at her notes while Geert storms angrily out of the room. In his haste, he almost knocks the usher over.

The female judge seems increasingly agitated and asks if the prosecutor wants to call any more witnesses to the stand. 'Not at the moment,' he says. The judge then asks Annet if she wants to call witnesses. She does.

Court is adjourned until the next morning, and then my witnesses will speak first. For now, I am free to go, but still on the condition that I don't travel and will report to court at 9:00am tomorrow.

The prosecutor still sputters that I should be put into custody, but the judges unanimously wave that off.

While eating the pizza we had delivered, we discuss my case. I express my admiration for the way Annet questioned Fenna and agent Geert. 'By the way, how did you know that this Geert has never filed any reports of rape or assault and that he was also punished for it, too?' I ask her.

'Just wait until tomorrow. Then I will call Chief Inspector Ria van Schoonhoven as a witness. Yes, that one,' she says, when she sees that I understand who she means. 'She'd love to tell us about how things were done at the Wibautstraat police station at the time and how frustrated our dear Geert is about his failed career. And that he's so keen to take revenge on one of those frustrated bitches who are to blame... Sorry, that's what he called those women – not me, you know.'

23 March, 2005 – Second day of session

At 9:00am we had reported to the Parnassusweg. At the entrance, I had seen Ria van Schoonhoven walking in. She was wearing a beautiful uniform today that seemed to have even more decorations on it than the last time I had seen her. She was clutching an impressive cap under her arm. When she had seen me, too, she had nodded in my direction. Gosh.

The public gallery is bulging. Not only journalists, I see, but also Bram, Edgar, and Greetje, some Spotty Nibblers, my colleagues from the Municipal Insurance Department, and also Johnny and his girlfriend. And then a lot of people I don't immediately recognize. The room buzzes with delight.

When everyone has taken their seats after the judges enter, a tense silence descends on the courtroom.

Chief Inspector Ria's testimony is brief but damning for Constable Geert. There really isn't a shred left of him. A feeling of euphoria takes hold of me. Gratefully, I watch her as she leaves the courtroom. In the public gallery behind me, people giggle here and there until the usher calls for silence.

After a quick Dutch lunch of bland cheese sandwiches and glasses of cold milk, the afternoon falls heavily on my stomach. Especially when they also want to ask me all sorts of thing.

I can't take it anymore, I'm suddenly completely confused as I stare blankly in front of me. 'Say, what?' I ask, when a few more questions are fired at me.

And then tears stream down my cheeks. A glass of water, hastily shoved at me, cannot calm me down. The audience begins to murmur, and after a consultation between the prosecutor, the judges, the court clerk, and Annet, the session is adjourned until 9:00am on Monday, 28 March. So, I have five days to calm down.

But I won't really get any rest. On the pavement in front of my apartment block, an army of reporters is waiting for me.

26 March, 2005 – In the papers

Carefully, I slide the curtains apart a little bit and look down. Nothing to be seen. To the left, right, and across the road, I can no longer see any reporters. People are walking towards the baker's, and students cycle out of town towards sports fields, forests, and parks. It seems like an ordinary Saturday morning.

Would the coast be clear enough to walk down the stairs to pick up the newspaper?

I sneak down the stairs and peak my ears on the landing. Do I hear anything? No, it's quiet. Quickly, I run down the last flight of stairs and yank everything out of my mailbox. With my loot wedged under one arm, I run upstairs, bang the door shut behind me, and put the two locks and the latch on my front door. My heart is beating in my throat, and I try to control my breath.

Even before I've completely calmed down, I'm startled by the phone. It's Bram, who anxiously asks how I slept. And whether I've seen the paper yet.

'See on page 3 of the second section,' he says. 'Please, take a moment to read everything and then call me back. OK?'

With a beating heart, I sit down at the dining table with the newspaper in front of me. At the bottom of page 3 is a modest article about my trial. 'Our court reporter' gives a summary of the first two days of session. The article concludes by saying that the session will resume next Monday and the verdict is likely to follow soon thereafter. My mouth is dry as I read it. Sweat pours down my back.

Only after reading the piece a second time, do I see that at the bottom of the article there is a reference to the Saturday insert. 'Read the whole story by our investigative journalist and judge for yourself (see the article 'VENGING ANGEL?' on page 3 of the Saturday insert).'

Among the pile of mail, I search for the Saturday insert with trembling fingers. After a deep sigh, I open it, and yes indeed: four whole pages.

Below the headline in big chocolate letters follows a slightly more detailed report of the first two days of court. Then they've printed a black-and-white drawing of me and Annet in the courtroom. I look like the criminal I am.

But below that drawing, the worst is yet to come. Here the reporter has included a nice mix of scraps and quotes from interviews that he has taken from everyone he could get in his sights. Nice for a juicy story then, but not so nice for me, I soon realize.

Fenna and Wieger sat down to paint a terrible picture of me; that, without a doubt, I have a murder on my conscience. And all because I couldn't stand it that the victim had found new happiness with his Fenna. Further down the page is a picture of Wieger, Fenna, and the beautiful, now 16-year-old Roberta in the middle.

My colleagues at the Municipal Insurance Department have unfortunately declined to comment, according to the article. But Constable Geert, now not restrained by a judge, speaks at length. Asked by the journalist why he has doubts about the cause of my father's death, he says that he has no doubts at all. I killed my father, and unfortunately we can no longer check anything with forensics because the victim was cremated very quickly. Nice coincidence, huh? But Mrs. Groenteman's witness statement is clear and I will not get away with it. He personally tracked down this witness, and then his colleagues from the investigation team were able to go to the prosecutor with a completed file. He is therefore confident that I will not escape my punishment. I read nothing in the article about the fact that it is a bit unusual for a traffic cop to investigate an alleged 1988 murder.

It is all very nasty. And his message still lingers a bit, despite quotes from an official statement from the Amsterdam police force, which refers to the testimony of Chief Inspector Ria, who states that no further announcements will be made about the case. The statement concludes by saying that Constable Geert has been suspended pending an internal investigation.

Some legal scholar, unknown to me, has doubts about my lawyer. He firmly believes that she cannot represent me properly because she is married to my brother and was therefore the daughter-in-law of the victim. And that is a little fact that Annet and I had so far managed to keep well hidden from the judges. Maybe the Dean should look into that, the scholar suggests. Especially also in connection with that story about those possibly stolen Krugerrands. Maybe my brother knows more about that.

Surprisingly, the ENT doctor who straightened my nose after the accident comes up. How on earth did they track him down? And I wonder the same about the comments from one of the ambulance paramedics who was at the scene at the time. Fortunately, he recounts what he saw: that I pressed shut the gaping wound in the victim's neck with my hand, even though I was injured myself.

Last to speak is a criminal lawyer. He specializes in vice cases. But from what he says, he does not defend the victims but only the (according to him, at least) falsely accused men. 'From his own practice' he digs up a number of examples of men whose lives were destroyed by women who had made the wildest reports.

Here, the journalist objects that in 1986, as well as later, no report was ever put on record. No, the man has to acknowledge that. It was just as well that no report was filed at the time. Yes, and look, he is not sufficiently familiar with all relevant facts to judge whether there had been any sex offense committed by the victim against the suspect at the time.

'Pfff, that's what you're coming up with now,' I think.

'But then again,' he undeterredly interjects, 'if there had been, then of course this in itself constitutes a strong motive for the charged offence of murder.'

Damn.

27 March, 2005 – Getting out

At four in the morning, I take one last look through a crack in the curtains to see if the coast is clear. I leave the curtains closed, and I have connected the table lamps to a timer. They will switch on and off neatly every evening, as will the television, which I've also connected to it just to be sure.

Through the kitchen window, I drop a backpack on the roof of the downstairs neighbors' extension. It is a nice bag from Rains, which Junior bought for me at the David Jones department store in Sydney. He sent it to me as a surprise package for my birthday. Way too expensive for the boy, but I was very happy with it, and now it comes in handy, too.

I hang the matching handbag diagonally across my chest, with 9,500 Australian Dollars and almost 1,750 Euros in cash stuffed into it. It is the last of the money from the *Banque de Luxembourg*, all of which I have now exchanged into valid currency. My almost new mobile is also in the bag, minus the SIM card. I took that out and put it in my old mobile which I left on my bedside table.

Finally, behind the zip of the small side pocket is my as yet unused blue passport, which features an emu and a kangaroo. I leave behind my bank cards, library card, and pretty much everything else that has my name on it. I only take my Amex gold card with me. That has my name on it, but no place of residence or anything like that. And although I don't intend to use it, I suspect it would be suspicious if I didn't have any cards with me. Imagine them searching my luggage! That's why I also put a used cinema ticket, a bus ticket, and Annet's old business card in my purse, along with the photos of Bram and Annet, my mother, and those of Edgar, Greetje, and Junior.

Carefully, I climb out the window and cautiously lower myself onto my black trainers, next to the backpack on the roof.

Since it's still dark, I reckon that in my black jeans and ditto winter coat, I will not be visible to anyone who might take a casual glance outside at this hour.

I sit still for a few minutes and hold my breath. Although it seems to me that I have made terrible noise, everything in the houses and gardens around me remains deeply peaceful. I reach up and gently push my kitchen window closed as much as possible.

Now it is important to reach the gate on Amsteldijk via the back gardens. If that can be done without anyone seeing me, I will be safe. Just before I reach the gate, a cat scurries into the garden path in front of me, meowing loudly. It's a hell of a noise, but fortunately no one reacts.

I am relieved when I feel the latch of the gate in my hand. With a dry click, I press it down and step outside. 'Praise and commend the fire brigade,' I think, by way of a quick prayer. Thank God they demanded that the door can be opened from this side without a key. After all, in case of fire, this is an important escape route for all residents, although they wanted the door to remain closed in order to keep uninvited guests (especially drug addicts) out of their gardens. So, a compromise had been struck. From outside you need a key, but not from the inside.

'Don't run and don't look around,' I tell myself as I step onto the pavement. At a calm pace, I walk through a still sleepy Amsterdam towards Sarphatistraat.

From there, I go to Schiphol airport, partly on foot, partly by underground, and partly by tram and train. Around seven in the morning, I reach the airport, which is already crowded. I hope I won't stand out too much among all those travelers.

In the ladies' toilets, I wash my sweaty hands thoroughly and freshen up. I also check how I look in the mirror one last time.

Without glasses and with my hair combed back, I look exactly like the ugly passport photo I had to have taken exactly according to the Australian embassy's specifications. Suddenly, I notice that the blue passport looks very new and unused. Carefully, I rub the concrete wall with it a few times and gently crack the spine of the booklet in a few places. I also fold some of the pages a couple of times and smear some eye pencil at the bottom of page. Now it no longer looks terribly new.

Satisfied, I go to the departure hall. There, I treat myself to a hot cocoa and drink it in small sips, sitting on an uncomfortable chair facing the Quantas desk which opens at eight o'clock. I put my backpack on the floor in front of me, with my feet planted firmly on it. I button my coat to the top and wrap my woolen scarf around my neck. Nice and warm, I yawn a little.

I dream about distant journeys I have never taken. For hours I can hover above travel guides and marvel at holiday paradises. I also always love looking at holiday snapshots of friends.

After Bram and Annet got married in 1991, I had suggested that Bram and I go to Australia together one day. After all, he had never been back. I had, but that hadn't been much of a success. Annet had raised her eyebrows when she heard of the plan and had sarcastically asked if she couldn't come along, but she eventually dropped any objections when she saw how much Bram and I were looking forward to it.

At the time, my mother had also reacted happily and enthusiastically when she heard of the plans. Although she had said nothing about our trip to Australia in 1985, she sighed often, very often, that she wished not only me but also Bram a really nice holiday in Australia. She was also quite willing to contribute to the cost, but she didn't have to.

Yet it had never happened. Bram and Annet both worked hard and had all kinds of social obligations beside their work that they could not or did not want to cancel at short notice. And applying for a visa took a lot of time. Once you finally had a visa, yes, you then had to go, because it was only valid for a few months. Something kept coming up. And when everything seemed to be in the bag, suddenly my mother had died.

In my dream I experience it all again. Half-awake on the uncomfortable chair, I shift slightly, trying to find a better position. The banister pokes nastily into my elbow. I register it but remain suspended in a state between waking and sleeping.

After much deliberation, Bram had decided that he would save for a sabbatical, during which he would be able to travel without disturbance, first with Annet, and then to Australia with me. That sabbatical was expected to be a reality in about ten to twelve years. And he had been proud of it, too, when he had told me.

But I didn't want to wait another ten years. Surely it had to be possible to leave earlier. I didn't want to be away from home for months either. A few weeks during the summer holidays would be more than enough.

By chance, I heard from a colleague at the Municipal Insurance Department that he had been to Nigeria with his girlfriend. He had had to arrange a visa for himself; 'quite a hassle,' he said. His girlfriend did not need a visa because, after all, she was Nigerian and had a Nigerian passport. I could tell from the photos they had had a very nice holiday.

It was only in the evening, when I sat with a large plate of pasta and the now customary stack of travel guides in front of me, that the penny had dropped. Of course, with an Australian passport, Bram and I wouldn't need visas! And then we could leave whenever we wanted.

In my dream, I see myself again walking past the International Court of Justice's building towards the Australian Embassy in The Hague. They hadn't been surprised by my request there, having studied my birth certificate thoroughly. Of course, I could have an Australian passport. I was Australian by Australian law because I was born there. *No worries!* I could have the necessary passport photos taken just around the corner, and for a fee of 150 Australian dollars I would have my passport sent to me by registered mail.

As simple as it seemed, it took a long time before something was finally delivered to me. I had already almost forgotten that I had applied for the thing, when a registered letter was suddenly delivered to me over four months later. I stared in disbelief at the blue booklet, which was valid for ten years. The ugly bitch looking at me from the passport photo was repulsive, and I convinced myself that I really didn't look like her. My surname was misspelled too, it said DeWit without a space. I had sighed deeply in disappointment and thrown the passport behind a pile of books at the bottom of the bookcase. Only last week, I had gone in search of the thing on all fours. It was supposed to be still valid for another two years or so.

27 March, 2005 – Take-off

With a jerk, I wake up when a trolley is being slammed against my leg. For a moment, I don't know where I am, and I look into the worried face of a man who asks me if I'm alright. Rubbing my leg, I assure the man with a hand gesture and a smile that nothing is wrong. At the same time, I glance stealthily at the digital clock above the Quantas desk. Oh no, it's almost nine o'clock already.

Quickly, I get up and get behind the short queue in front of the desk. After only a few minutes, it's my turn. A ticket for Sidney is no problem.

'One-way or return?' asks the lady behind the counter. I can tell from her accent that she's Dutch and hope she won't hear that I don't exactly have an Australian accent either, as I say 'one-way, please'. Stubbornly, I continue to speak English and so does she. She glances only briefly at my passport.

Then she gives me the choice of flying tomorrow, or the day after tomorrow, via Singapore. But I can board a flight via Dubai later that afternoon. Then I must stay there for a night and stopover. I get a last-minute discount of 25% with this option.

'Fair dinkum,' I say with a broad smile, hoping she will understand that this Aussie girl wants to go for the latter option. And she does. Within a blink, she puts a nice one-way ticket for me on the counter and doesn't look surprised when I pay the 850 Euros in cash. She wishes me a pleasant journey and briefly points to the ticket, which says somewhere that I must report to the Quantas check-in desk in departure hall 2 at 2:30pm at the latest.

Since I still have time, I go back to Schiphol Plaza, where I buy a suitcase, a bunch of new summer clothes, a few colorful scarves, new underwear, a beauty case with contents, a couple of books and magazines at various shops, a pair of sunglasses, a couple of sets of disposable contact lenses, and also a new summer jacket, with the remaining Euros.

In the toilets where I have been before, I put on a completely new outfit and I swap my glasses for lenses. With a little fiddling and tears, it works, just like at parties where I, out of vanity, hadn't wanted to show myself with glasses. I strip the price tags off the purchases which I cannot put on right now. Then I stuff everything, old and new mixed up, into the new suitcase. I push the price tags and receipts into the sanitary bin.

Finally, I walk slowly towards the departure hall. I check in at a quarter past two without any problems. The suitcase and the rucksack go as check-in luggage, and the beauty case can go as hand luggage, on the condition that my small handbag will fit in it during boarding. And it does.

At a quarter to five, the Boeing 747 pushes off from the gate. As the plane takes off for the six-hour flight, and I see the Netherlands getting smaller and smaller below, I wonder if I will ever see it again.

28 March, 2005 – Doubt in Dubai

I've checked into the first hotel I came across at Dubai airport, because I didn't feel like going through customs. Seeing the city was not what I came for either.

The prepaid SIM card that I've bought for 50 Australian dollars from a telecom shop in the arrivals hall is still in its plastic wrapping on my bedside table. This afternoon at three o'clock local time, my flight to Sydney will depart, and I have to report to the check-in desk an hour beforehand.

It is now a quarter past ten here, two hours later than in Amsterdam. Annet will probably be nervously wondering at this moment where I am, because in fifteen minutes I am due to report to court.

I do feel bad about doing this to her. What if I never saw my family and friends again? Did I do the right thing in running? From sheer stress, I haven't been able to eat breakfast yet. Only the coffee I drank. The caffeine gave my heart rate another boost.

Chewing on one of Junior's far too sweet, hard mints, I think about calling or texting Annet. I don't know exactly how it works, but I'm pretty sure she doesn't have to cooperate with the police if they were to search for me.

With some fumbling, I put the SIM card in my mobile and send her a text message saying that I feel bad and will stay in bed today. 'I'll call you later,' I end the message. Then I wait nervously until it's one o'clock. I hope Annet will be back at the office in De Bilt by then.

She answers with, 'Is that you, Kiki? Hell, where have you been? How sick are you?'

'I'm not sick, I just had to leave. I've no intention of being locked up. That one night in police custody was enough for me.'

'Jesus, Kiek, what kind of nonsense is this? Your case is not doing badly at all. I really think the chances of you being convicted and going to prison are very small. Don't fuck it up now. I've told the court you're sick. And they didn't like it, to say the least, but the session has already been postponed, until next Wednesday this time. When you're back by then, it won't matter that you've run away.'

'I cannot be back by Wednesday, it's impossible.'

'You mean you don't want to be. Can't you see you're not doing yourself any favors with this kind of stupid action?'

'It just can't be done. In time, I mean. I'm too far away for that now.'

There is silence at the other end of the line. But after a few seconds, Annet asks, 'So where are you? Surely, you can't have gone that far in that short a time. And without a passport.'

'Without my Dutch passport, I couldn't have. But I also have an Australian passport.'

I hear her breathing rapidly into my ear, as if she's panting after a good run.

'Kiek, no!'

'Annet, sorry, a thousand times sorry, but I was panicking. I do not want to go to prison for something I don't feel guilty about.'

Again, there is silence at the other side – a long one now. 'I'll get back to you as soon as I can,' I say, and quickly disconnect before Annet can say anything more.

At a quarter to two, I stuff the croissant still lying on my breakfast tray into my mouth and pour the fresh orange juice after it. I stuff the apple and the plum, wrapped in a napkin, in the beauty case.

Trying not to think, I register at the check-in desk in the nick of time and wait for my connecting flight to Sydney to depart. While waiting in line, I quickly text Junior:

> Arriving tomorrow at 10:02am,
> Sidney airport, flight EQ412, come meet me
> there if you can. Love, Auntie.

I ignore the many notifications of missed calls. At the gate, I turn off my mobile and pensively bite into the plum.

29 March, 2005 – Welcome home!

After fourteen hours of flying, the Airbus lands with a bang on the runway of Sydney's Kingsford Smith International Airport.

I awake with a startle and am completely disoriented when, out of the windows, all I see is the water on both sides of the runway. I even think for a moment that we have crashed into the sea. Only after the flight attendants have walked through the cabin from front to back with large aerosol cans spraying insecticide, do I come to my senses a little. The lemon smell makes me a little queasy. Or is it the nerves?

Cheerfully, one of the flight attendants chirps through the intercom that we should be patient for a while, as we are yet to be linked to a gate. The local time is 10:00am and the temperature is a crisp 18 degrees Celsius, with a forecast of 20 degrees and some rain for later in the day. Oh yes, it is autumn here. Quickly, I fill in the incoming passenger card – the form for customs that the flight attendant had placed on my lap. In a hurry, I tick all the multiple-choice questions.

From the beauty case, I pull out one of the colorful scarves I bought in Amsterdam and wrap it around my shoulders. That will have to do.

I step out of the plane tense, with the apple in my left hand and the beauty case in my right. In the long queue of passengers, I walk through the arrivals hall towards customs. It's overwhelming to be here again after such a long time.

I join the queue for Australian passport holders and try to appear as casual as possible. It helps that I can occasionally take a bite of the apple and chew on it.

When it's almost my turn to show my passport, out of the corner of my eye I suddenly see a large shepherd dog approaching. He sits down right next to me, stiffly waiting for his handler – a man in a uniform that says 'airport security' in big letters across the front and the back.

'G'day, ma'am, can I see your incoming passenger card?'

'Sure,' I say, and hand the thing over to him as my knees buckle.

With sarcastically raised eyebrows, he points to the box I've ticked 'yes', next to the question whether I have fresh fruit with me. Then he looks at the half-eaten apple in my hand.

'Shit, sorry, sir, I wasn't thinking,' I say with my mouth full.

He finds it amusing and points to one of the large rubbish bins, specially set up for dunces like me to dump food that is not allowed into the country.

Then it's my turn at passport control. The customs officer feels at a few pages and scratches over something with his fingernail. Then he quickly looks at my passport and me in turn a few times and types something on his keyboard. He had watched amusedly as I had made a fool of myself with my apple.

'Oh, the joys of jet lag,' he chuckles. Then he folds the passport and hands it back to me.

At the baggage carousel, I kill time with my phone. It takes me a while to turn it on and pair it with an available network. Immediately, several notifications of missed calls from Annet appear.

Earlier than expected, my suitcase and backpack pass by on the belt and I manage to pull them off just in time. Dragging them along, I walk with the line of passengers towards the exit. But before I reach it, I have to put my luggage on a stainless-steel table and unzip it. Two customs officers then rummage through my clothes. The man is mostly interested in the contents of my suitcase and backpack. The woman looks at my toiletries in the beauty case; she even smells the bottle of shampoo. She also looks in my handbag and gestures that she wants to look in my purse. Everything I have to put on the table, including my mobile, which suddenly beeps.

I've received a text message from Junior:

Waiting for you at taxi booth outside terminal 2.

The customs lady reads the message. 'From my nephew, he's picking me up,' I say.

She smiles kindly and hands me back the device. I am allowed to go through. '*Welcome home!*' she says.

30 March, 2005 – Acting stupid

Junior is overjoyed to see me but also very anxious, even worried. In his small room in the hostel where he is staying, he is anxious to hear what is going on. As tired as I am, I tell him how I left the Netherlands and how I prepared my trip. I can see he doesn't get it. But he also seems to find it exciting that I'm on the run, like an action hero in a thrilling film.

He insists on Skyping with his parents with me. I sit dog-tired in front of his laptop to call Edgar and Greetje from their beds. But they are soon online.

Actually, I don't have to tell them much new, because they have already heard from Annet that I am travelling with an Australian passport. It was immediately obvious to them that I would be travelling to Australia, to Junior. But they bit their tongues and didn't tell Annet that Junior is in Sydney, though they found it hard not to be completely open with her and Bram. They will continue to stay away from the court. They wouldn't be there for the time being anyway, as I'm supposedly home, sick in bed.

I can see they're quite angry that I'm involving Junior in all this. They implore me to stay under the radar here on the other side of the world – an Australian among other

Australians. During one of their many Skype sessions yesterday, Junior told them that I had sent him an English-language text message via a new mobile number, so they had understood that was indeed my intention. And how long will I stay there, forever maybe? They'd really rather I didn't stay with Junior too long. Even Edgar doesn't look as friendly as usual.

But Junior pushes me into his boy's bed after the talk. It smells wonderfully familiar, and I fall into a deep, dreamless sleep.

When I wake up again after a few hours, Junior is sitting in the office chair, looking at me thoughtfully, and I realize how stupid I am to burden such a young boy with my presence here. I'm a fugitive, and he's actually still a child who should be having a good time here.

'Have a nice sleep, Auntie Kiki?' He slides a glass of juice across the desk to me. Sitting on the bed, I empty it in one gulp.

'Um, I'm not allowed to have guests here, and no visitors are allowed after eight o'clock either. Besides, I also have to work tonight at the pizzeria. Shall we see if there's another room for you?'

'No, dear, a hostel isn't for me; it's more something for young people. And besides, it's better if I'm not too close to you. I need to find a place of my own. What time is it?'

Junior looks at his watch. 'Almost half past two now.'

An internet search yields a short list of cheap hotels in a three-kilometer radius from the hostel. We agree that I will leave my luggage with Junior for now, and that I will work down the list myself. At a quarter to eight at the latest, I will return to collect my luggage.

I don't dare to use the communal shower in the corridor, so there's nothing left but to go out with my handbag on my shoulder, unwashed. Oh well, I'm not going to be in a four-star hotel anyway, and I've just come from the airport. They'll forgive me for looking a bit disheveled.

The first two hotels on the list have no rooms available. The third does, but it is on a busy road. The fourth hotel only has a very large, overpriced family room for me. Undecided, I stand on the pavement, while traffic hoots busily and pedestrians walk past me. I have already walked quite a bit and I am hungry. First, I have to get something to eat and drink.

In a side street, I find *Joe's Place* – a small restaurant, where I eat a delicious salad at a bar in front of the window and drink a glass of the Barossa Valley white wine. The little restaurant is otherwise almost empty, and that suits me fine. My feet hurt from walking, and I stare dejectedly at my list of hotels. Should I go to that hotel on the busy street again?

The waiter – a nice guy, by the way – brings me another white wine, looks over my shoulder at the list, and asks, 'Looking for a place to stay?'

I explain to him that I will be staying in Sydney for a bit longer. 'To do what?' he asks me somewhat cheekily, yet not intrusively.

'To write a book.' I make it up on the spot. 'My first one, so I'm on a bit of a budget and I need some peace and quiet.'

He subjects me to a cross-examination. He can hear from my strange accent that I have lived abroad for years. And then he asks whether I just want a room or a whole flat. Whether I will receive guests, be willing to clean and do some chores myself, whether I will make a lot of noise, and so on. It's a barrage of questions.

Apparently, he is satisfied with my answers, because he shouts loudly to Tanya, the restaurant's cook. This small woman of around fifty, with spiky jet-black hair, appears to live in the flat over the restaurant. And there's one little room left there.

After some bargaining, we agree that I can live in that room for a month, if I clean the flat (including Tanya's room), do the laundry, take care of breakfast, and finally pay a two-hundred-dollar deposit and then a hundred dollars cash every week to the landlord. And that happens to be Joe, the owner of the entire property, whom I mistook for the waiter.

Outside, he shows me the way to an ATM, assuming I don't have that much cash with me. For form's sake, I walk in that direction. After five minutes, I'm back at the restaurant to hand him two hundred dollars from my purse. He makes a copy of my passport, sends me a text message so we have each other's mobile numbers, and hands me a set of keys without me even seeing the room.

'And no catfights!' he says to Tanya in warning. She just sticks her tongue out at him and walks back to the kitchen.

Joe explains that the kitchen help suddenly left two weeks ago, and that Tanya is having to do everything in the kitchen by herself. Finding a replacement for the kitchen help is not that easy, because the restaurant is not running very well and he cannot offer a high salary. If I can take over some of Tanya's household chores, hopefully she'll be able to hold out for a while longer, especially if he can also give her a little extra out of my rent.

Upstairs, I look around the corner of what will be my room for the next few weeks. A bed, a wardrobe, a wooden chair, and a bedside table with a small mirror above it. That's all there is. And it's all that will fit.

The kitchen is surprisingly large and opens onto a balcony, which overlooks a courtyard. In the middle of the kitchen is a large, wooden dining table with four chairs, and in the corner is a small red sofa in front of a big television. The kitchen is impressive, with all kinds of appliances. It's also filthy. Fortunately, the bathroom and toilet are fairly clean.

I call Junior with the good news and ask him if he can buy some good granola, tasty coffee beans, and some fresh fruit somewhere, because I couldn't find any of these in the kitchen. I then make my bed with the sheets I find in the closet. Lastly, I put all the dishes in the dishwasher, clean the counter, and quickly run the vacuum cleaner through the entire apartment.

Quite chuffed, I walk to the hostel. Together with Junior, I lug my luggage and groceries to *Joe's Place* and introduce him as my nephew from the Netherlands. Joe shakes his hand warmly and doesn't bother us as we walk up the stairs to the apartment at the back of the restaurant.

4 April, 2005 – Judgment

ECLI:NL:RBAMS:2005:2822/33
Authority: District Court of Amsterdam
Date of judgment: 04-04-2005
Publication date: 06-04-2005
Case number: 28775-1

Criminal law
Content indication:
Acquittal of the murder and robbery of Mr. Robert de Wit

Excerpt:
District Court of Amsterdam
Team: criminal cases, no. 1
Number: 15/10-00157-2
Date of judgment: April 4, 2005

Judgment by the District Court of Amsterdam, three-judge chamber for criminal cases, in the case against the defendant:

- **Kiki de Wit, born in Port Augusta, Australia on 25 December, 1965,** residing at 288-III Stadhouderskade in Amsterdam

Counsel for the defense: Master A. van Rijn, lawyer in De Bilt.

Court proceedings:
Considering the arguments and evidence presented to the Court during session on 22, 23 and 30 March, 2005.

Indictment:
The defendant has been charged with what is stated in the summons. The text of the summons is annexed to this judgment.

Prosecutor's position:
Master M. Beers, prosecutor, has demanded:

- Judgment against the defendant on the charge of premeditated murder (Count 1), or unlawful killing (Count 2);
- Judgement against the defendant on the charge of theft from the victim (Count 3) at the time of the aforementioned act (either Count 1 or Count 2);
- Imprisonment for a period of at least 6 years.

Prosecutor's arguments:
It has been argued that it can be legally and convincingly proven that the defendant deliberately and premeditatedly

took the life of her father, Robert de Wit, or committed the act of unlawful killing of her father Robert de Wit, at the time of a car accident on 4 March, 1988, and that she robbed the victim of a minimum of four (4) Krugerrands.

There is legal and convincing evidence to convict the defendant, based on the statements of witnesses, the other relevant circumstances, and because the defendant has not unequivocally refuted several striking circumstances prior to and surrounding the death of her father.

Judgment:
The Court decides that it has not been proven that the defendant is guilty of any of the charges and **acquits the defendant on all counts.** An extensive acquittal consideration with regard to the report of the municipal coroner, the reliability of the witness statements, the lack of supporting evidence for those statements, exculpatory facts and statements, and the plausible alternative scenario of the defendant is annexed to this judgment.

This judgment was rendered by:
Master J.H. Janssen, chairperson, and Masters B.A. de Vries and F.W. van den Eikelenburg, judges, in the presence of Master F.M.H. van Bergen, court clerk, and delivered at the public hearing of this Court on 4 April, 2005.

7 April, 2005 – Relief

Speechless, at the kitchen table I read on my new laptop the judgment that Annet has e-mailed me that afternoon. I'm so stunned, in fact, that I cannot even be happy.

After a cup of strong tea, which I drink standing at the now shiny countertop, I sit back down at the table and read through everything again.

Tanya pokes her head around the corner of the kitchen door. 'Hard at work?' she asks me with a wink. But she doesn't wait for an answer and I hear her walking down the stairs to the restaurant, where she's preparing for dinner.

When I no longer hear her, I immediately click on the Skype icon and on Annet's picture. Apparently, she's waiting for me, because within a minute she's online. Bram is standing behind her, and he smiles broadly at me.

'Hey, Kiek, the coast is clear. Are you coming back home soon now? I miss you.'

'Wait a minute, I'm overjoyed of course, but is this really all true?'

'Yes,' says Annet dryly. 'You are exonerated, really. Not guilty on any of the charges. Maybe you should come home now, after all. How long did you think you could fool everyone with that story that you are sick in bed at home? The prosecutor could still appeal, but I don't expect him to do so. So, you can consider the judgment as final.

'You are officially innocent of murder or unlawful killing, and that so-called theft has not been proven either. And they don't know you fled. If that had been a criminal offense, then that is no longer relevant now, although you will probably have some explaining to do if they find out. And so will I.'

'Wait, wait, wait, not so fast. What exactly did you say about that prosecutor?'

Annette sighs audibly. 'He could appeal the verdict within 14 days.'

'What does that mean? Then I have to go back before the court again, if he appeals?'

'Yes, before the High Court. But don't worry, the man really won't. He had to go through so much dust when the last witnesses had told their story, he will not put himself through that again.'

I swallow hard. 'Sorry, but you're going too fast, I must have missed something.'

Bram nudges Annet and takes her place in front of the camera.

'That article in the newspaper caused a stir. The nurse from the AMC hospital, who I saw at the time when you were waiting for me in the corridor, told Annet everything. And that ambulance paramedic has added to his statement. All in all, little, in fact nothing, remains of the prosecution's case. And Fenna and Wieger, they looked like fools. Just like that cop, by the way. What was his name again?'

'Geert.'

'Yes, that's the one. None of them want to speak to a journalist anymore, ha-ha, the cowards.'

I am quickly trying to think of what options I have. I can hear Annet and Bram shouting louder and louder, but I need some time to come to a decision.

'OK, then I'll stay here for a while,' I say after a few minutes. 'First, I want to be sure that the prosecutor won't go for an appeal.'

'What utter nonsense, you can't do that,' Annet says angrily. 'You should just come back now. There was already no need for you to leave for the other side of the world so suddenly. And you wouldn't be safe there if they put out a warrant for your arrest either. The Netherlands has had an extradition treaty with Australia since 1985, you know.'

'Yes, nice. Maybe it's all indeed highly emotional and irrational what I'm doing, but *hey,* this is all I can think of doing right now. And even though I miss you all terribly, I can't do anything in the Netherlands anyway. I'd better make the best of it and do some sightseeing over here for the next couple of weeks.'

We argue for a while longer. It soon becomes clear to Annet that I won't change my mind, and I see her walking out of the room in frustration.

I can see Bram does understand my decision. He glances over his shoulder to see if the door of the room is really closed. 'I, um, understand now what happened then,' he says.

My heart skips a beat. 'Okay,' I say. 'It might be better if we never talk about it.'

I see that he doesn't dare look at me, just nods in agreement.

April 2005 – *Walkabout*

Almost every other day, I Skype with Annet and Bram. They are always short conversations. Annet is still angry, I see; Bram avoids looking straight at me.

I keep in touch with Edgar and Greetje via Junior's laptop. I don't want to call, Skype, or text them via my own mobile or laptop, so that no one else can find out where I am and I don't unwittingly involve them further in my troubles.

Other than that, I take a lot of short trips around Sydney and the surrounding area. Sometimes Junior joins me, and then we make a fun day of it. For example, we go to a show at Sydney Opera House together. But mostly, I go out alone.

I tell Tanya and Joe that I am going to get inspiration for my book. They don't really care what I do. Tanya is happy with her clean apartment, her freshly laundered sheets and towels, and her tasty breakfasts. When we bump into each other in the kitchen, we just have fun. Joe, in turn, is pleased that Tanya is so happy and working hard in the kitchen of his restaurant. Usually, he or Tanya give me some tasty snacks from the kitchen for my dinner.

I walk and walk all day, more and more relaxed, and more and more like an Australian among the other Australians. It has a calming, almost therapeutic effect.

Actually, I have already completely relaxed when I receive a text message from Annet halfway through the month:

Prosecutor will not appeal!

I answer:

OK, I'll be back! Dates and so on to follow. Kiss.

1 May, 2005 – Return journey

Quickly, I look around and sniff the air before I climb the flight of stairs to the Singapore Airlines plane which will take me to London Heathrow via Singapore.

During the flight, I think back to the special time I had in Australia. Despite everything, the last week there was perhaps the happiest time of my life so far. As I look out the plane window, I try to imagine what it would be like if I lived in Australia permanently.

It is only after the hectic transfer at Singapore's immense airport that I fall asleep. I dream about my trips with Junior, the accident, my mother's death, my work at the Municipal Insurance Department, Edgar and Greetje, Bram and Annet's wedding day; everything in one big, confusing mess. A few times, I wake up and eat and drink something from what has been put on the unfolded table in front of me by a flight attendant. But then I sleep again. As a result, the journey seems short.

We land at Heathrow in the dark, and we taxi towards the gate in the pouring rain. The journey towards baggage and passport control seems almost longer than the flight. Tired, I line up under the Commonwealth Passport Holders sign. I pass passport control in the blink of an eye, without being asked a single question or given a glance.

Once I have passed customs, I look around, searching. There is a huge crowd, waiting eagerly behind a bar fence for friends and relatives. Only after I've walked along the fence for a third time, tense, do I hear Bram shout, 'Kiki, over here!'

He stands waving wildly at me. Relieved, I run towards him as quickly as the heavy suitcase I have with me allows. How good it is to see him again. I'm definitely not going to live in Australia, I'm sure of that now.

During our extended, emotional greeting, I whisper in his ear, 'Are we two OK?'

'Definitely,' he says, looking straight at me.

'By the way, I have what you asked for here.' He taps his breast pocket. 'Annet picked it up from the police yesterday. And I moved the curtains in your living room and that green vase on your windowsill again. From the street, it looks just like you're at home.'

Together we travel by taxi to Harwich, where we will catch the ferry to Hoek van Holland. As an Australian, I was able to fly to the UK without a visa. However, to be able to travel on to the Netherlands unnoticed, I need my Dutch passport at embarkation. Bram conjures it from his breast pocket, along with his own passport, at the right moment.

That very evening, I am home in Amsterdam.

Epilogue

My life ripples on. Nothing special has been happening for years, and I am quite happy with that. I am content with my boring job at the Municipal Insurance Department, happy with my family and friends, and I feel good in my own house. The fewer unexpected things happen, the better I feel.

Once a year, I take a four-week holiday. Then, I go to Australia. I always visit a different city to explore, and from where I make short trips in the surrounding area. I often meet Junior somewhere. He has since built a life in Australia with his Julia. Together, they run a travel agency.

I also once took a bus trip through the Nullabor Plain. Amazed, from my comfortable seat I watched the beautiful, red landscape that passed by me.

I try not to think about all that happened years ago. That seems to work, but sometimes unpleasant childhood memories suddenly present themselves to me, like uninvited guests who refuse to be sent away.

On the advice of a psychologist, whom I occasionally see in connection with persistent sleep problems, I write down everything about these uninvited guests in a notebook. But without emotion, factually, and as if it were about other people and I could watch quietly from a distance, in the third person. When I light the fireplace in winter, I use the pages from that notebook to light the fire.

Because I am turning fifty today, Bram and Annet, together with Edgar and Greetje, have organized a party for me. And I'm gathering courage for that by the fire I stoked that afternoon.

There will be good food, no doubt. It is Christmas, after all. None of the guests are churchgoers, but good food is part and parcel of this day. And combined with my birthday, it will be a double celebration. So, everyone responded enthusiastically to the invitation. For some, I am sure, it is also nice that this arrangement means they have to forego gloomy Christmas dinners with family. I am personally a little less enthusiastic.

But although I don't really feel like it at all, I try to imagine that a big birthday party could also be fun. And I trust that my demand that no Sarah doll appears on the scene will prevent the worst horrors.

So, after a long delay, I put on my nicest clothes and resignedly let myself be transported in the taxi to a jetty on Rokin. There, a guard of honor by the guests awaits me at a canal boat, hired especially for the party.

About the party, I can be brief. It's fine, but I'm just not much of a party person. I like seeing everyone and having a good meal. But for me, it didn't need to happen in such a massive gathering.

My Uncle Hans comes and sits next to me and says to me in a confidential tone, 'Never mind. You got that from your mother. She didn't like it at big parties either.' Alcohol fumes hit me in the face.

'Oh, that must have had something to do with your father, too,' he says, snuggling up to me. 'He always wanted to keep up appearances for the outside world at parties and celebrations. What a truly horrible guy he was. He was my brother, yes. But that just needed an egg from your grandmother, and a sperm from your grandfather. And hey presto... Nasty man, is all I can say.'

He takes another firm sip from his glass of wine. With apparent pleasure, he then whispers wetly in my ear, 'And she's dealt with him nicely, anyway. Managed to get rid of him in the end.' He takes another sip.

I look at him in surprise. 'What do you mean?'

'That night, when she went to check on you at the hospital, didn't she inject her whole syringe of insulin into him? There you go. And good riddance, I say.' And then he falls asleep with his head on my shoulder.

****

Author's note

The main characters in this book are fictional, I made them up. Many people will share likes, dislikes, quirks, and maybe even nasty traits with the main characters. But if, as a reader, you recognize yourself in one of them, then that is a coincidence.

Domestic violence was long seen as a marital problem, a private matter in which few people wanted to get involved and in which the police often intervened, only when it was already (far) too late. In the Netherlands, the first safehouse for battered women and the right to welfare benefits for divorced women did not appear until the 1970s. Dutch police now record about 84,000 incidents of domestic violence every year. This is probably the tip of the iceberg. Out of shame or fear, many victims do not report the crimes committed against them by their spouses. And I find it terrifying to think about the numbers worldwide.

While writing, I took some liberties with Dutch criminal law and Dutch court proceedings. Here and there I adjusted the course of events during the described court case so that the story flowed smoothly. For example, criminal trials usually take much longer (sometimes years), and there is much more time between the days in court and the judgment than I assumed for the sake of the story. The 18-year statute of limitations for murder in the

Netherlands was dropped on 1 January, 2006. The bill was obviously pending long before that, but I ignore that in this book. I did stick with the Dutch non-jury trial system.

Incidentally, I have placed the story against the backdrop of historical events and facts from the 1960s onwards. For example, emigration in great numbers to Australia actually took place; emigrants were shipped across the globe as in the story, and the Bonegilla migrant camp really existed. I took some details about this from the stories of my own parents' emigration to Australia in 1963.

KB
Baarn, the Netherlands
March 2023

Milton Keynes UK
Ingram Content Group UK Ltd.
UKHW011810080823
426544UK00001B/84